# MONTSERRADO
## Stories

## *Also by Ophelia S. Lewis*

2014 - Dead Gods HM2
2013 - **Good Manner Alphabets (how to be a super polite kid)
2011 - Heart Men (a novel)
2011 - The Dowry of Virgins and Other Stories
2009 - **A is For Africa
2009 - **The Good Manners Alphabet Book
2007 - Journeys (a collection of poems)
2004 - My Dear Liberia—Recollections

**CHILDREN'S BOOK

Readers of this book are encouraged to contact the author with comments;

E-mail: ophie2020@yahoo.com
Author Website: www.ophelialewis.com
facebook.com/ophelia.lewis

Village Tales Publishing provides traditional publishing services and turnkey services to individuals that seek to successfully self-publish and promote their books. We handle all aspects of publishing—editing, design, production, marketing and order fulfillment.

Please visit our website:
www.villagetalespublishing.com

# MONTSERRADO
## Stories

### Ophelia S. Lewis

VILLAGE TALES PUBLISHING

NORCROSS, GEORGIA

www.villagetalespublishing.com

## Print and eBook
Available from Amazon.com and other retail outlets
Available on Kindle and other devices

Print Paperback
ISBN: 978-0-9853625-0-8
Library of Congress Control Number: 2012943891

eBook
eISBN: 9780985362546

Printed in the United States of America

## *Dedication*

In memory of Mariah Pupoh Ross, my cherished friend, who taught me that happiness is never being wrapped up in success or possessions, but in the concerns of others. Mariah lived her life well, acting on her spiritual beliefs conscientiously by helping those in need. Meeting Mariah was like receiving a gift; she left fingerprints of grace on many lives, especially mine.

# Contents

# *From the writer's pen*

Whether you believe in God or not—this is true for people everywhere—life is a painful mixture of good and bad. So where do people go for help when struggles and pain threaten to shake their life and steal their last ounce of joy? For those who see the world through the filter of faith, it is not odd to consider that no human has absolute power to turn his or her life around without God's help. The "Believer" leans on God's hope.

This book comes to publication at a very important time, when Liberians and people throughout the world are rebuilding lives and dreams. While I have elected settings in four counties in Liberia—Montserrado, Lofa, Margibi and Maryland—it is with honesty (and human-heart) I've tried to galvanize the emotions of personal and spiritual struggles of everyday people in Liberia. Of course, these emotions are similar for people throughout the world, regardless of ethnicity.

Each story attempts to show hope through the human-spirit after the civil war in Liberia. The characters may make you laugh or cry, but it's sure to make every reader experience the human side when faced with life's challenges. Each story stirs the reader to a realization of the opportunities God's providence may bring to the weakest of the weak.

In **Good Father** (Lofa County), you will see the role of three men in the life of a young man's realization of his dream; a coach who recognizes the boy's potential, a father, whose molding of his son is threatened by what he considers an empty dream and a grandfather, whose voice of wisdom evokes reasoning. Tamba Sawie wants to be a football star. However, Kallon would rather his son acquire farming skills to be a good provider for his family. Oldman Galakpai believes his grandson does not have a lazy spirit, which the boy's father is convinced of, just a different one.

A moral lesson pervades the story in **Firestone** (Margibi County) when the instrument of deliverance is unconditional love. Empathy is least expected when a 15-year-old boy is elevated from a life of crime to a normal life where opportunity awaits him. Firestone is caught breaking and entering the Bah's home. Rather than taking him to prison, his victim is offering a different path.

Although **Sweet Mother** (Montserrado County) is a pure work of fiction, I wanted to write a story that would be impossible to forget, and in doing so, honor Liberians that lost everything during the civil war—life, dignity, hopes and dreams. The real life occurances these characters face, one can not conceive a more dramatic, surprising series of events. The fate of two strangers collides when a rape victim of the war, Sundaymah Boye, with no desire to improve her life, and Nick Anderson, a thirty-something year old African-American who is losing his life to cancer, meet. What each has to offer one another is priceless.

Finally, in **Believe** (Maryland County), the Almighty humbles the proud and exalts him when he begins to trust. The providence of faith in God is strikingly displayed as divine power is united with human effort—the means used is human; the deliverance is divine.

I hope you find as much contentment within these pages as I had writing them.

*Ophelia S. Lewis*

*Acknowledgments*

God is first in my life; I know who holds the future and I know who holds my hand.

My tender love—always—to my mother, Jeanette Lewis-Harding, for her love, support and encouragement.

I cannot begin to thank my family who makes so many sacrifices for me each day; Aaron, Marie, Veronica, Joann, Akitee, Derick and all my children. You are always so willing to alter your lives to accommodate my needs.

Nadia Assaf-Cole, I love you in truth, my friend.

It is a struggle with every new project, trying to make ends meet. Every time I think I've made ends meet, it seems someone or something moves the ends. No amount of words is ever enough to express my gratitude to these individuals. The value of your support bringing this book to print is immeasurable; Nazira Dendy, Manseen Logan, Lemriel Logan, Dr. Tim Nevin and Carol Nevin.

Finally, I am extremely grateful to Bella Beau Marketing & Publicity, LLC for the superb job in advancing my work. You guys are the best.

My dearest brother, Jenkins N. Lewis, Jr., no amount of words can describe how much we've missed your presence. This void can never be filled.

"One life on this earth is all that we get, whether it is enough or not enough, and the obvious conclusion would seem to be that at the very least we are fools if we do not live it as fully and bravely and beautifully as we can."—**Fredrick Buechner**

**Note:**[1]

---

1       *The information on playing soccer is intended for general information purposes only and should not be considered to represent official or sanctioned specifications. Please consult your league, organization or sanctioning body for their specific dimensions and/or diagrams.*

# Good Father

Tucked away in Foya District, about forty-one miles from Voinjama[1], resides the tiny village of Chakporma, a parish of about ten huts. Chakporma is rich with laughing children and friendly neighbors. The entire village shares one man's troubles just as his achievements are celebrated by all. Western culture is odd here, a world without modern conveniences. Life is simple as there is neither electricity nor running water. The huts are raised slightly above the ground, most built round with mud walls and splendidly topped with dried palm thatch. Some are even built with roofed verandas along the outside to accommodate the family during their leisure moments and, at times, neighbors who have come to visit. Nearby each hut is an opened shed which is used as the kitchen. It is a neat little area where a cooking fire, distinctive by three stones, strategically placed triangularly to support cooking pots over the hot coals.

Kallon Sawie, a prominent member of Chakporma, alone cultivated three cassava farms—one newly planted, well-tilled in rich soil with good drainage, one yielding and the other in recovery, but still yielding—and every year harvested not less than one ton (2,000 pounds) of cassava from each of his farms. The Liberian government did well for him when they gave him his first cassava stalks free. Kallon left goat herding; hoping his oldest son, Tamba, would take over while he did the farming, which he felt could lead the family to a prosperous life. Cassava grows easily and grows fast, and not much

---

1    *Capital city for Lofa County, one of fifteen counties in Liberia, West Africa*

fertilization is needed. But Tamba had disentangled himself from his father's affairs, attending school at the public institution in Hundonin, the nearby town. This was against Kallon's disposition of course. It is Tamba's mother who insisted that he attend school.

"If the boy would only hear me, he would understand he is seeking only a dream," Kallon complained to himself. "How can he get a wife if he is not able to do his own farming?"

Kallon grieved over his son's ill-consideration of attending school as alternative to farming or goat herding. Tamba had hardly given either a try. Kallon went on complaining, not realizing how fast the day had passed, until the griping noise his stomach made let him know Borbor was late in bringing his food. Then he heard the boy.

"Papa! Papa!"

He looked up and saw Borbor standing by the farm-kitchen[2] at the edge of the cassava patch, with a tray balanced on top of his head. Kallon dropped his hoe and hurried toward the shack. He met Borbor soaked with sweat, breathing heavily and smiling.

"Did you bring some water?" Kallon asked, slightly annoyed. Then he took the tray off the boy's head, placed it on a bench and mumbled, "You will forget your own head had it not been attached to your shoulders."

There was only one time Borbor forgot to take water with his father's food, but Kallon would never forget it. Since that incident, each time Borbor delivered the food, Kallon reminded the boy with the same insult. Sensing his father's anger, Borbor hesitantly peeled the decanter strap off his shoulder and handed the bottle to Kallon.

Kallon grabbed it out of frustration, unscrewed the cap and drank. "Why are you just coming?" he asked as soon as the decanter left his mouth.

"I was waiting on Mama…she was talking with Aunty Sia," Borbor said, placing the blame on Finda.

Kallon sucked[3] his teeth. He knew the boy had been playing on the way, which was the main reason for coming late. He uncovered the dish and his lips parted with a satisfying smile. Finda had traveled to her husband's heart without a doubt. The bowl was full with

---

2     *A shack built with four long posts and roofed with slanting palm thatch. Some cooking is done here while people are working on the farm, but it is mainly used for taking breaks and eating lunch.*

3     *To hiss*

steamed new[4] rice and beans-torborgee[5] submerged in fresh palm oil, packed with meat and dried fish. Borbor giggled childishly to his father's cheerful expression.

"Have you eaten?" Kallon asked.

"No," Borbor shook his head.

"Let me see your hands," Kallon demanded.

The boy reluctantly opened his hands, showing dried mud stained on both palms.

"You were playing...that's why you were late," Kallon said, pointing an accusatory finger at the boy. "When will you learn? I have told you, *A boy, whose hands are clean, will eat with kings.*[6] Your hands are filthy. I would have invited you to eat with me, but this will be a lesson. I will not share this food with you," Kallon shook his finger in the boy's face. "Go and sit over there," he pointed to a stool in the farm-kitchen.

Borbor's gaze fell to the ground. Then he hung his head and ambled to the stool. He sat down without lifting his head, actually a little disappointed or even angry with himself for not checking his hand before reaching the cassava patch. Feasting on the best portion of the family meal was an exclusive privilege that delivering Kallon's food offered, a much-anticipated reward for walking almost two miles to the farm.

Using a calabash, Kallon dipped water out of the bucket and washed his hands. Then he sat on the bench, opposite Borbor, and begun eating. Every time he loaded his spoon with food out of the bowl and fed his mouth, he glanced at the boy. It was mainly to see Borbor's mood, whether he was pouting after being scolded. Borbor looked more miserable than angry, supporting his chin with both hands, staring down at the floor.

Kallon calmly said, "Go and wash your hands."

The young boy whisked off the stool, hurriedly dipped water out of the bucket and scrubbed every trace of mud off his hands. Then he hurried to Kallon and waited for the official invitation.

"Let this be the last time I tell you to always be prepared," Kallon

---

4    *Locally grown rice, recently cut, dried, and beaten in the mortar*
5    *Torborgee has three types: Pepper Torborgee, Beans Torborgee, and Bitter-ball/ Kitili Torborgee. The sauce is often made with pea-like vegetables (pea-eggplants) extremely bitter in taste, but when prepared, the flavor is enjoyable. Torborgee is associated with Liberians in the Northern part of Liberia, mainly, Lofa County.*
6    *African proverb*

lectured. "You may not always be given a second chance. Okay?"

"Yes, Papa," Borbor mumbled.

"You can eat with me," Kallon invited and handed Borbor the extra spoon.

Borbor shoved his spoon into the bowl, scooped up some rice and anxiously stuffed his mouth. "Papa," he said, chewing and smiling.

"Yes, Small-man," Kallon answered. This is what he calls Borbor when he is in a joking mood.

"May I stay here with you today?" Borbor asked.

Kallon was happy to hear such request coming from his youngest son. The words were sweet in his ears. Unlike Tamba, who would have run back to the village to play football[7] rather than help him on the farm, Borbor had offered to help. As far as he was concerned, Borbor had done more than his share for a nine-year-old. From the time when he was able to walk to the cassava patch alone, Borbor happily took on the task of carrying his father's lunch. The boy had done well, except for a few occasions when he came late. Kallon even praised Borbor openly, purposely to stir some jealousy in Tamba's heart so he would rather work on the farm than go to school or play football. Tamba always chose school so he could play ball with his friends after school.

"What would you do if I allow you to stay?" Kallon asked.

Borbor boasted, "I will help you."

"Are you going to work hard?" Kallon asked, only joking.

"Oh, yes, Papa…I will work very hard! I will dig up the biggest cassavas," he said, spreading his hands far apart.

"I see," Kallon said, pleased. "When we are done eating, gather your mother's dishes and then you can help me."

They had eaten close to seventy-five percent of the food when Kallon put down his spoon and left the rest for Borbor. He drank water from the bottle, making sure some was left for the boy, and walked back to the cassava patch to continue his work.

Kallon had not resumed his work long when a rattling noise, more like the clatter of dishes, broke his concentration. He looked toward the farm-kitchen and saw Borbor gathering them together.

"Be careful," Kallon yelled. "No wonder your mother is always complaining about the chipped enamel coating on every dish she has sent me."

---

7    soccer

"Yes, Papa," Borbor said and went slower.

The clattering noise stopped and in a short while Borbor joined his father. He mimicked Kallon's progress while he harvested the cassava, lifting the swollen roots and plowing the same soil into small mounds to which selected stems were put in.

"I plant new stems while the soil is still loose…to replace the cassava with a new one to grow," Kallon explained.

"I see," Borbor said and followed. "Papa, is that why we always have a lot of cassavas?"

"Yes," Kallon nodded. "You are learning something that is very important, my son. You will be a clever man when you grow up."

"I'll be like you, Papa," Borbor beamed.

Kallon and his little helper pulled up and broke off many swollen roots and placed them in bags. Each place where the roots were pulled, Kallon aided the spot by another bit of hand plowing and planted new stems. Borbor followed at a child's pace.

"Small-man, you've worked very hard," Kallon said to the boy, sensing the weariness of Borbor's hands. He was hardly moving now. "It is time for your break."

Borbor asked, "What about you, Papa? Isn't it time for your break too?"

"Not yet," Kallon chuckled. "But, your help has practically carried the day's work to its end. I can finish the rest of it by myself. Go and rest."

Borbor beamed with pride, happy to have carried part of his father's labor. He dropped the bag he was holding and hurried to the farm-kitchen.

"If only you were Tamba's age," Kallon muttered. "I wish Tamba and Borbor would switch their age so Borbor is older."

Borbor had not left the cassava patch more than five minutes when Kallon heard snoring noise coming from the farm-kitchen. Borbor was on the pad, lying on his side with both hands tucked between his knees, sleeping.

"Farmwork is exhausting for a man, much more a young boy," Kallon said to himself. "Tomorrow, it is Borbor who will be a strong man."

Kallon's labor requires a great deal of energy as the day passes slowly under the weight of the heat. Near dusk his own pace had gotten slower, as if heavy iron was on both arms and legs. Kallon pulled a rag from his trouser pocket and wiped his brow to end the day's work. While he cleaned his hoe and cutlass, he wondered about what happens when Tamba sits down for a meal. Whether he thought about his father who labors in the hot sun so that he, Tamba, could eat such delicious meals. Kallon had to harvest one ton (2,000 pounds) of cassava to make $100. The entire family benefited equally, but Tamba was not part of the solution in the way Kallon thought he should be. Kallon put his tools away and then woke Borbor so they could go home.

\*\*\*\*

They had barely reached within hearing distance from the village when Kallon heard his wife's quarrel. He suspected she was screaming at no one other than Tamba Sawie, who might have come home late again. Wearied from his work, Kallon took his time until he reached the kitchen.

Finda was standing directly in front of Tamba—one hand resting on her hip, the other pointing an accusatory finger at his face—while he stood staring at the floor.

"What has he done?" Kallon asked as soon as he entered the kitchen. "Or should I ask, what has he done, again?"

"Tell your father!" Finda hollered. "Tell Kallon you have lost all of my money! Tell him how you were too busy playing football you did not care to look after my bread money!"

Finda's rice bread, crafted down to the bare basics, may be simple but it is not easy. Every ingredient is processed from scratch and then baked in a cast iron pot over fired charcoal. Over the weekend, Kallon and Tamba collected enough firewood for the week while Finda produced the rice-flour[8].

The time from oven to delivery is never less than three hours. Finda starts the fire four hours passed midnight, before mashing ripe plantains and bananas in the mortar to add to the rice flour. All thirty-six tin cans[9] are greased, to facilitate the easy removal of the finished muffin, and set aside. When all the ingredients are mixed, she pours

---

8    *Rice powder made from finely milled rice. Raw rice is grinded or beaten to flour, in a mortar with pestle, and sifted.*

9    *Carnation milk cans used as muffin baking pans; both top and bottom ends are cut off the can to form a ring, 9.5in circumference and 3in height, giving the rice bread a round cup shape.*

it into the tin cans halfway, twelve at one time, in the cast iron pot and sets the pot over the fired charcoal. The heat produced from the charcoal cooks the bread, which takes a minimum of forty minutes to cook. Regulating the temperature is tricky. Fired charcoal is placed on the lid and underneath the pot, which Finda manipulates to the end of cooking. Too little heat underneath, and the cast iron pot will cool; too much, and the bread will scorch. No timer is set, doneness is judged by eye.

At twenty-five cent each, Finda earns $4.50 every day; that is, if Tamba sells all eighteen muffins in his breadbox[10]. Six muffins are set aside for the family breakfast. Kallon takes two to work, Finda and each of the children gets one. The balance twelve muffins get sold in the village, mostly on credit.

Tamba stood quietly, not knowing how to position his body so he would not present the wrong body language. He dare not portray a pout and worst, he did not have a rebuttal. Every penny made from selling the bread was unaccounted for. Also, the last time he tried to explain the reason for coming home late, while Finda was yet quarreling, a fast slap crossed his lips to remind him when either of his parents was talking, he was to remain quiet. It was rude and disrespectful, on the child's part, to talk while the adult was still speaking. Although Finda continued to scream, Tamba did not repeat that mistake.

"Tamba, is that so?" Kallon asked angrily, still trying to remain calm.

Tamba lifted his head but did not utter a word.

Kallon screamed, "Is that so?"

Not only did the boy look lazy, he looked dumb in Kallon's eyes.

"The money was in my pocket the whole while," Tamba muttered.

Kallon furrowed his brow and eased his anger. "Were you playing football," he asked, calmly.

Answering truthfully meant admitting he'd been playing football. Tamba remembered Kallon's strongest warning the day before. He stood quietly.

"Tamba, answer me," Kallon warned. "Were you playing ball?"

"Yes, Papa," Tamba admitted quietly, "it was after school." He prayed his answer would make a difference and added, "I attended

---

10    A 25" x 20" rectangular case typically constructed with three sides wood and one side made of acrylic glass for clear displaying of bread, pastry, etc. when selling.

all of my classes first."

Kallon looked at the rattan[11] laying on the table and heaved a heavy sigh. The cane, an appalling reminder to all misbehaved African children, seemed a reasonable measure for Tamba's behavior. However, worn-out from his farmwork, there was no energy left in Kallon to lecture the boy, let alone use the stick. In fact it had been a while since the cane was used as punishment for Tamba. By eleven-years-old he had grown a foot taller than both Finda and Kallon. Neither one had admitted to it, but the boy's height had promoted him from beating to lectures. Since he turned fifteen, Tamba was expected to take on some adult responsibilities, but Kallon had been lenient because of his school. Now Kallon had grown tired of the boy's carelessness.

"You behave as if you and Kumba were the same age," Kallon scolded, humiliating Tamba in comparing him to his five-year-old sister. "In fact, I think she does more work around here than you do."

Finda chuckled at her husband's silly discipline, as in taunting amusement, though she understood his fatigue. Her husband works hard.

"I am sorry, Papa," Tamba mumbled. "I promise to do better."

"Isn't that what you said the last time?" Finda asked. "Tamba, your promises are always empty." She cut her eyes at the boy to show disastisfaction of his behavior.

Tamba looked at his mother, read the disappointment on her face and hung his head. He wished he'd not hurt her so badly, then he would have told them how he was a hero on the football field today, scoring the winning goal, and how his teammates carried him away on their shoulders. Without trying to suppress any of his guilt, tears filled his eyes and rolled down his face.

"Tamba's dream is a lazy man's dream," Kallon accused the boy to his face. "In fact, it is your mother's dream that you are ending, not mine. She wants you to be an educated man, but I want you to be a man. I want you to be someone who is able to feed his family. I am not an educated man, but I feed my family well. Do you not eat well?"

"Yes, Papa," Tamba mumbled.

"Then Tamba, what kind of man are you going to become?" Kallon scolded.

---

11    *Cane or rod used for beating / flogging (treatment to correct or punish, as in to discipline)*

Tamba stood mute.

"Very well then, starting tomorrow you will go with me to the farm. You will learn to be a *man,*" Kallon laid his judgment.

Tamba looked at Finda, who usually intervenes each time Kallon threatens to take him out of school. This time Finda did not seem eager to beg on his behalf. Instead, she looked away.

"Please, Papa...I promise to do better," Tamba cried. "I swear, Papa...I will do better."

"No! No!" Kallon answered. "Tamba, it is my responsibility to teach you to be a man. Tomorrow, when you are not able to feed your family, the blame will be on me. That is my final saying. You will go with me to the farm, starting tomorrow morning."

"Tamba, go and help Borbor and Kumba," Finda interrupted before Kallon said another word. "Take them to the washroom."

Kallon suspected his wife was intervening, but waited to make sure of it.

"Yes, Mama," Tamba muttered and dried his face. Then, gathering the children, holding each by a hand, he led them to the washroom.

As soon as the children were out of hearing distance, Finda said to Kallon, "You were only scaring the boy, were you not?"

That confirmed his suspicion.

"No, Finda, I am serious," Kallon replied. "I am tired of his carelessness."

"What about his school?"

"Tamba does not want to go to school to be educated. He goes there to play football. What would he accomplish playing ball? I do not want him to become a lazy man, Finda. The boy has to learn to work hard. Why can't you see it?"

"Kallon, the boy is careless, I will agree...but he does well in school," Finda pleaded. "Taking him out of school will hurt his chances. Tamba's education will be good for the whole family. He can help Borbor and Kumba."

"I cannot believe we are having the same argument," Kallon muttered. "It is not Tamba's dream, it is your own dream. Tomorrow, when Tamba turns out to become a lazy man, people will blame me, not you, his mother. In fact, what dreams does Tamba have? He does not have a dream of his own."

"Have you asked him?"

"I do not need to."

"Tamba has a dream," Finda argued. "My son will be the first educated man in Chakporma. He will bring light[12] to our village."

"It is you who have put all these things in the boy's head," Kallon accused his wife. "Let me tell you something, Finda...it will only poison his capabilities. Watch my words. Because of this so-called dream, Tamba will become the laziest man in Chakporma. He will not be able to take care of his own family. This will shame you...no, not you... me...not just me...us!"

"You are wrong, Kallon," Finda pleaded. "My son will become an educated man. Tamba will learn all the book[13] we did not learn."

They heard the children running toward the kitchen before Kallon had the chance to rebut.

"Mama...Mama!" Kumba was habitually calling her mother like most five-year-olds.

The children reached the kitchen, holding hands. Finda forced a smile, abandoning their argument, and walked away. Staring at his wife's back, Kallon sucked his teeth in protest, but purposely out of hearing, otherwise she would have returned. Finda always had the last word in their arguments.

The three children sat on self-assigned benches while Finda served the dinner she had slaved over. The crackling fire was warm and pleasant, overriding the argument that Kallon and Finda had not ended, yet no one seemed willing to talk about the events of their day. Kallon would have told them that Borbor asked to help him on the farm and how hard he worked for a young boy his age. Tamba would have told how his teammates carried him on their shoulders when he scored the winning goal and everyone would have laughed. Imagine Tamba sitting on the shoulders of *fools*, Kallon would have thought. Perhaps even Kallon would have chuckled. But Tamba's carelessness had made the family dinnertime doleful.

When everybody was finished, Kallon quietly walked out of the kitchen and headed to the washroom. Tamba collected all the dirty pots and pans, washed them and put them away in their proper place.

---

12    *Electricity*
13    *Education*

Next, he collected the three kerosene lanterns, removed their globes, and gave each a sparkling shine. Tamba trimmed their wicks and filled each lamp with enough kerosene for the night.

Tamba did all his chores without Finda reminding him of any of it. It seemed as if he had turned over a new leaf in one night. Tamba did more work in a single night than he had done his entire life, it seemed. He did everything right. Kallon could not help but notice the boy's bustling performance when he returned from the washroom.

"Why are you smiling?" Kallon asked his wife, who was obviously happy that he'd noticed Tamba's performances.

"Look at your son," Finda pointed at Tamba as he was now filling the water drum by the kitchen. "Tamba is making sure that I have enough water to use in the morning without me asking him."

"It's like putting fire on a turtle's back," Kallon said. "Maybe Tamba needs drastic measures to do the right thing."

"I love you, Kallon Sawie," Finda coaxed, in a soft voice.

"Yes, Finda, he can go to school in the morning," Kallon said, correctly reading his wife's mind.

Finda raised her arms and hugged her husband's neck to celebrate his change-of-heart. "Thank you, Sawie, you will not be sorry," she whispered. "I believe Tamba is going to do better."

"I swear, Finda, this is the last chance that Tamba gets," Kallon warned.

"Yes," Finda assured.

"I mean it," Kallon warned again, this time softer.

"I know, Kallon Sawie, I know. I'll make sure Tamba know this. You have always given him second chances. He, too, has always promised to do better. I think he means it this time."

"We will see," Kallon mumbled and left it at that.

The evening had started awkwardly, but it ended harmoniously. Tamba reacted to his second chance with jubilation, despite the strong warning Finda added. Kallon had come to the end of his rope, she told him, so the boy's promises were to be kept no matter what.

****

Tamba woke up before Finda the next morning. He took his bath, got dressed and even started the fire for Finda to make her rice bread. Then he cleaned the breadbox and padded it with a clean towel. Everything was done without anyone reminding him. Finda was happy when Tamba carried the breadbox to the kitchen while Kallon was still in the kitchen, getting ready to leave for work. The timing was good; Kallon will see that Tamba had turned over a new leaf.

"Remind Borbor to bring me some drinking water," Kallon said to Finda, purposely ignoring Tamba. He picked up his cutlass and the two pieces of muffins Finda had put aside for his breakfast.

"Did Borbor forget to take some yesterday?" Finda asked.

"No," Kallon said. "I don't want him to forget."

"Okay," Finda nodded.

"See you in the evening," Kallon said to his wife and walked out of the kitchen.

Finda stacked the eighteen muffins neatly in the breadbox, thinking to herself whether or not to remind Tamba of his promise.

"You must try to sell all the bread today," Finda said to Tamba instead. "This money will be used for next week's market[14]."

"I will bring all of your money today, Mama," Tamba promised.

"All right, Tamba," Finda replied, "Please make sure of it."

She helped Tamba balance the breadbox on the top of his head, making sure the front acrylic side faced frontward. Tamba picked up his notebooks, tucked them under his armpit, and started to leave. School was a two-mile walk away.

"You must come straight home today after school," Finda reminded him anyway.

"Mama, I will," Tamba lied, knowing an important football practice had been scheduled for today.

Finda fed her two small children their bread and got ready for her customers from the village. Rain or shine, Boakai, Finda's best friend's husband, was her first customer.

"Good morning Finda," Boakai greeted. "My wife has become lazy because of your bread. Had it not been for its taste, it would mean trouble for her," Boakai put his true feelings into a joke. He handed her seventy-five cents.

"Sia is not lazy," Finda said, taking the money. "She does this to patronize me." She wrapped Boakai's order, the three muffins he paid

---

14      *In this case, it is reference to grocery needed, and purchased from the marketplace; like salt, rice and those not from the family vegetable gardens.*

for and dashed[15] him an extra one free. "Tell Sia that I say, '*hello*'," Finda said and handed Boakai the delicious warm bread.

"Thank you," Boakai said, forcing a smile. He took his package and walked away.

Finda had no problem selling the rest of the rice bread. In fact two other customers came after she had run out. It was the ones Tamba took with him that worried her. Selling the bread was easy; keeping the money safe was hard.

Finda prepared lunch for Kallon and asked Borbor to take it to the farm, also reminding him to take some water. Then she went to the nearby creek to do the family laundry. After hanging the clothes out to dry, she started the evening meals. By late day, Finda had completed her cooking, picked up the clothes, folded them, and put them away. With barely enough energy left, she took her bath and got ready to greet her family.

"Kumba," Borbor shouted as he and Kallon entered the yard. "Look at what I have for you!"

Kumba jumped off her mother's lap and ran to meet him.

"I brought you this," Borbor said and handed his baby sister a tangerine.

Kumba grabbed the tangerine and ran with it to Finda. She handed Finda the fruit, hoping she'd peel it.

"You can eat it later," Finda said, taking the fruit and placing it on the table.

Kallon reached the kitchen shortly and read Finda's face, it looked worn and exhausted. Her wrinkled brow proved her feelings to be unsatisfactory also.

"Where is Tamba?" Kallon asked, knowing well enough his assumption of his son staying after school is never wrong.

"He has not come home," Finda answered, frowning. Her voice had more anger than worry.

Kallon only grunted his intense disapproval of the boy's defiance. He quietly put his tools away and headed to the washroom.

Finda served her two small children their dinner, in silence, and then set Kallon's dinner on the table. Kallon returned to the kitchen thirty minutes later, dressed in clean clothes.

"Tamba is late," Kallon exploded, as he entered the kitchen. "This

---

15   *A bit of something added, free to customer*

is the straw that has broken the camel's back."

Kallon met no resistance. He did not care to recreate the last conversation he'd had with his wife about her son—yes, now it was her son—and his lack of owning some type of responsibility. It is Finda who is pampering Tamba's childish behavior. Kallon expressed his thoughts to himself.

"Get your father some water," Finda said to Borbor, who by now had his hand covered with red palm oil from the food he was eating. "Never mind," she mumbled and went to get Kallon's cup with water. "Don't let Tamba spoil your dinner," she pleaded to Kallon and placed the cup on the table.

Kallon ate his dinner quietly. In his mind, he gathered his thoughts of what exactly he was to tell Tamba when or if he came home. For once he was certain Finda would not intervene. He had waited long enough for this chance.

The beam of a car headlight suddenly flashed inside the kitchen. Kallon put down his spoon and watched the Land Rover drive close up and stop. A white gentleman, tall and lean, stepped out from the front passenger door, and then Tamba got out of the SUV from the back passenger door. Kallon instantly noticed his son did not have the breadbox with him. The car lights went out and the engine died. And then, the driver opened his door and stepped out. Kallon recognized the school principal, Kaifa Londo, as he hurried to catch up.

Kallon had his eyes locked on his son as he and the stranger entered the kitchen. Catching his father's glare, Tamba did not know whether he should start explaining or wait. He saw Kallon's lips move, but no sound came out. Tamba cleverly turned to Finda.

"Hello Mama," Tamba mumbled, scratching his head because of nervousness. "Sorry I'm late."

"Now he has lost my breadbox…can you believe it?" Finda whispered to Kallon.

Kallon kept his peace, upholding politeness in front of their unexpected guests.

"Good evening, Ma Sawie," Kaifa Londo greeted Finda in the Kissi language and shook her hand. "Mr. Sawie," he also greeted Kallon, "How are you?"

"Good evening, Mr. Londo!" Kallon replied, in Kissi, and shook Kaifa's hand.

"Mama, this is Mr. Muller...he is from America," Tamba introduced the stranger in English.

"Ar-melic-ka!" Finda said in simple English. She'd never met anyone from America. "He is very tall," she said in the Kissi language. Then, in simple English, said, "Hi-lo, Mista Muller."

"Ma'am," Ryan replied, smiling and shaking Finda's hand firmly.

Ryan released Finda's hand without the snap-popping noise Liberians make with their hands when they end a handshake. Finda smiled and quietly walked away to give Kallon's dinner proper storage. Kaifa introduced Ryan to Kallon, in English, and the men shook hands.

"Please, sit don," Kallon said in simple English, and pointed at the two available benches. Then he asked Kaifa, in the Kissi language, to interpret all conversation further. He felt his simple Liberian English was not impressive enough to communicate his thoughts clearly.

Kaifa told Ryan of Kallon's request and Ryan nodded.

"Mr. Sawie, I must first apologize for keeping Tamba so late. It is my fault," Ryan said and sat down, which Kaifa interpreted.

"Tamba should have told you that if he is not home at a certain time, his mother worries," Kallon said; Kaifa interpreted.

"I understand and I am sorry about that," Ryan said.

Kaifa interpreted and added he too was sorry and hoped Kallon would understand. Kallon nodded it was okay.

"Papa, Mr. Muller wants me to play football for his team. He said I will be paid," Tamba said, in Kissi, holding back his excitement.

Kallon heaved a heavy sigh, keeping his temper calm. He was right all long; football is behind his son's deliberate misbehavior. "What about your school?" Kallon asked calmly, trying not to seem rude before his guests. "Who will sell your mother's bread?"

Kaifa asked Kallon's permission to interpret to Ryan the conversation between Kallon and his son. Kallon allowed it.

"Mr. Sawie, this is a once in a lifetime opportunity," Ryan said cautiously. "Tamba could be taken into the ODP."

Kallon furrowed his brow. He had no idea what the man was talking about.

"The ODP is a program that helps young people develop their talents to participate in the Olympics," Ryan explained.

Kallon continued frowning.

"Let me explain," Kaifa said to Ryan and then explained in the

Kissi language what Ryan was trying to say.

Kaifa explained, the ODP—Olympic Development Program—is the start of the identification process for the National and Olympic Teams in most countries. The purpose of the program is to identify players with exceptional talents and develop them to represent their country's national team, Lone Star[16], for instance. Eventually, most of the players are hired by professional clubs and are paid generously for playing football.

"With players like Tamba, Lone Star team will shine for us," Kaifa exclaimed, in English.

"Tamba's talent can send him places," Ryan added, "I've watched him play. He has speed, a great first touch and natural ability to score goals."

Kaifa interpreted, word for word.

"Sorry, Mr. Muller, I do not understand any of it and I do not care to," Kallon said.

Kaifa interpreted.

Ryan collected his thoughts before speaking, careful not to offend the man. "Mr. Sawie," Ryan continued, "I identify players of the highest caliber on a continuing and consistent basis. This will lead to an increase in success for the Liberian National Team. Your son will benefit even if Lone Star does not reach the final rounds. Tamba will be exposed to international coaches, coaches who are there looking for talent...like Tamba's."

Kaifa interpreted.

"Mr. Muller," Kallon said, raising his palm. "I will be impressed if you tell me Tamba can make an entire rice farm by himself or if Tamba can plant half of the amount of cassava I've planted or if Tamba can mind the herd of goats other boys his age, in Chakporma, mind."

Kaifa was ending his interpretation when Finda returned, joining the men.

"Is Tamba in some kind of trouble?" Finda asked her husband in Kissi language.

"No, but we are," Kallon said to her in Kissi.

"Uh?" Finda said, looking at her husband. She could tell from his face Kallon was keeping his feelings under control because of the guests. "What is going on," she asked anyway.

---

16     *Liberia's National Soccer Team*

"Your son has decided to throw away his life," Kallon said, looking at Tamba.

Tamba caught his father's stare and looked away.

"Go on Tamba...tell your mother what you and Mr. Muller have told me," Kallon grunted.

Kaifa interpreted to Ryan the exchange between Kallon and his wife.

"Mr. Muller, I am sorry," Tamba apologized.

"Tamba, don't give up so easily," Ryan encouraged the boy. "Let's give your father a chance to hear us out."

"I am sorry if my son has encouraged you to come," Kallon apologized to Ryan and asked Kaifa to interpret. "He should know better."

"I understand your concern, Mr. Sawie. I, too, have a son," Ryan said, after Kaifa interpreted.

"Does he play football rather than go to school?" Kallon asked; Kaifa interpreted.

"He is only four," Ryan said, smiling. "I hope he is as talented as Tamba."

Kaifa interpreted.

"Mr. Muller, do you see our village?" Kallon asked, pointing out the darkness. "We have no electricity or running water here. All these things that we need, our big government has not given them to us. Do you see my wife? She believes that Tamba will give them to us. That is the reason she has taken him from our farm which feeds my family. My wife dreams one day, when Tamba becomes an educated man, he will do all these things for his village. Now, you are asking me to allow him to leave his school to play football? Have you come to ask me to help end my wife's dream?"

Kaifa interpreted Kallon's speech, word for word.

"Mr. Sawie, you have every right to feel this way," Ryan replied. "If I was in your shoes, and Tamba was my son, I would feel the same way."

Kaifa interpreted.

"Then why are you here? Have you not come to ask me for Tamba to play football?" Kallon asked.

Kaifa interpreted.

"Yes," Ryan replied.

"Who gets paid for playing?" Kallon chuckled sarcastically. "Only children play. Even they don't get paid for that."

Ryan chuckled at Kallon's sense of humor after Kaifa's interpretation.

"If my son had the talent that Tamba has, I would let him follow his dream," Ryan said.

Kaifa interpreted.

"Dream? Tamba wants to play as if he is a child. What man feeds his family by playing? Mr. Muller, my son will go to school. If he chooses not to, then he will go back to helping me on the farm. I will not allow Tamba to play football as if he is a child. Tomorrow when he becomes a man and is unable to feed his family, I will be blamed."

Kaifa interpreted, shrugging his shoulders.

"Mr. Sawie, if I were to tell you that Tamba will continue to go to school while playing, would you allow him to join my team?"

Kaifa interpreted.

"Tamba plays football against my wishes now while he goes to school. It is because I have been easygoing...listening to my wife. I intend to put my foot down before things get out of hand," Kallon said.

Kaifa interpreted.

"Please, let me explain to you what I mean, Mr. Sawie," Ryan pleaded.

Kaifa interpreted and Kallon nodded.

"Your son is talented," Ryan explained. "As far as I have seen, he is the best footballer in this country and he hasn't even been trained by a coach. When Tamba develops his skills, people will pay him a lot of money to play football. He can give you all these things that you have named if he takes advantage of the opportunity."

Kaifa interpreted.

"What about his school," Finda interrupted. All she'd heard was, football...football...football. "I want my son to go to school. I want him to become an educated man."

Kaifa interpreted.

"He will go to school as long as he wants to," Ryan said. "I will make sure of it. Tamba will continue his education while he plays ball."

Kaifa interpreted.

"When will he sell my bread?" Finda asked. "How can Tamba sell my bread, play football, and go to school?"

Kallon grunted while Kaifa interpreted for Ryan.

The persistence of his uninvited guests meddling in his family's affairs was starting to set annoyance. Kallon stood up, but decided not to ask them to leave.

"If Tamba wants to throw his life away, it is his business," Kallon said in a decided tone. "I will not contribute to it. If he wants to behave as a child, it is his life. God is my witness, so no one can blame me. I have done all that I can do for my son. Tonight, I will not help him throw away his life. Let him do as he wishes," Kallon finished and walked out of the kitchen.

Kaifa interpreted for Ryan.

"Where are you going?" Finda asked.

Kallon waved his wife off and continued walking; past his hut, across the yard.

"I know where he is going…to my father-in-law's house," Finda said, as if obligated to tell the guests of her husband's destination. Kallon had not excused himself properly.

Kaifa interpreted. Then, he suggested to Ryan they give Kallon time to think things over.

"Mrs. Sawie, I am sorry if I have caused trouble in your home," Ryan apologized. "If what I have told you is not true, I would not be here. Your son has a special gift and if he uses that gift to his advantage, he will be able to help you."

Kaifa interpreted.

"My husband does not see it that way," Finda replied.

Kaifa interpreted.

"Maybe I should give him time to think about it," Ryan said. "This is an opportunity for Tamba…a chance for a bright future. I know your husband wants the best for his son."

Kaifa interpreted.

"My husband is a hard worker," Finda said. "But no matter how hard he works, he is not able to bring light here or build a concrete[17] house for me and his children to live in. If he was educated, maybe he could have done it."

Kaifa interpreted.

"Kallon feels he has failed his family," Finda continued. "He knows he can never disappoint me, I've told him that. But he does not want Tamba to be in his shoe. Tamba and I should help Kallon on the farm; instead Tamba goes to school and I wake up at four every morning to

---

17    *House built with cement*

make bread to sell so I am able to buy books and uniform for Tamba's school, besides the small-small things we use around the house."

Kaifa interpreted.

"Mrs. Sawie, I want to help Tamba," Ryan said. "That is the only reason I'm here. He is good…very good."

Kaifa interpreted.

"I know that, Mr. Muller," Finda chuckled and said, "Tamba has been bouncing anything that resembles a ball on his head. He kicks everything out of his path, as if it was a ball. Tamba made his own ball out of dry[18] rubber when he was seven-years-old. He used to follow the rubber tappers even against our strong warnings. Do I care if Tamba plays football? No. If Tamba likes to play football, there is nothing I can do about it. All I care about is he attend school."

Kaifa's interpretation brought on a smile to Ryan's face.

"I'd like for your husband to hear what I have to say," Ryan said. "Do you think if I come back tomorrow he will hear me out?"

Kaifa interpreted.

Finda collected her thoughts and said proudly in simple English, "Yeah…I go tel he you dey com tomoro."

"Thank you, Ma Sawie," Ryan said, trying his best to speak like a resident of Chakporma village.

Finda liked that; she let out a girlish chuckle.

\*\*\*\*

A light breeze was blowing across the village. The setting was calm and lovely with just the quiet mutter of neighbors' ongoing conversations. Another day had ended, just another beat in the slow rhythm of existence in Chakporma. Kallon did not care he had left his guests without properly excusing himself. His people are friendly and hospitable and they always show gracious ways to outsiders, especially to a westerner such as Ryan Muller. In this case his guest had become a frustrating reminder of Tamba's bold defiance.

Walking hurriedly, Kallon advanced toward his father's yard, to where the family had gathered around a campfire in the kitchen, talking about life. Galakpai Sawie could tell from his son's face he was not happy. Kallon greeted his eighty-three-year-old father and the others, and then he sat down on a stool next to him.

---

18   Latex

"Tamba behaves as if he does not have an ounce of Kissi blood in him," Kallon complained. "It is hardly easy for a Kissi man to be so lazy." Then he put his head in his hand and moaned, "I don't know what else to do."

Kallon's spirits seemed more broken than his voice made known. He had not come for small talk. He needed words to reason with his son, Tamba Sawie, words that would not push him away. Old Man Galakpai did not say a word, but his heart and priorities were visible to Kallon—a gentle, positive, silent support.

An incredible bond had come between Kallon and his father the year he was unable to work. It was because of the weakness of his body after the malaria[19] attack. He had already lost most of his crop when they became infested and he had no money to spray. Kallon endured extreme hardship that left him penniless and his family's life nearly in ruins. It was Galakpai, his old father, who picked up his hoe and worked row by row to remove the strangling weeds that constantly threatened the few cassava crops that had remained. Galakpai worked alone throughout the day, regardless of the stifling heat or battering rain.

It was clear Kallon had come to ease his grief. Family members politely excused themselves to give the old man personal time with his son. Just Galakpai was left with his son so Kallon could speak his mind freely.

"This American man…a stranger, is telling me what is best for my son," Kallon said. "Imagine that. I've been struggling to teach Tamba about hard work while the man is telling me playing ball will make my son a responsible man…he must take advantage of their opportunity. I shook his hands, Father…our women's hands are callous compared to his."

Galakpai giggled at his son's sarcasm, then asked, "What exactly is he saying? What about school?"

"Tamba will attend school while he plays ball," Kallon mumbled.

"I like the school part," Galakpai said. "So what exactly is bothering you, Kallon?"

"What worries me is how poorly my son is fitting in our village,"

---

19     An infectious disease characterized by recurring attacks of chills and fever, caused by a protozoan of the genus Plasmodium in red blood cells, which is transmitted to human by the bite of an infected female anopheles mosquito.

Kallon admitted. "Especially, Tamba's lack of interest in farming or herding goats. It is my responsibility to teach my son, but Tamba copes with hard work by playing. That is not the way it should be."

Galakpai Sawie simply sighed.

"Father...I've allowed myself to be embarrassed in front of our people. I'm now paying the penalty for my leniency."

"Embarrassed? What are you embarrassed about?" Galakpai asked. "Tamba does not steal...he goes to school and one day he will be a big[20] man in all of our eyes. I thank God that none of my sons have a drinking problem."

"We work hard like you, Father. Since our *biriye*[21], we've all worked hard."

"You work hard, Kallon, but not like me," Galakpai corrected respectfully. "You are different."

"Different?"

"Yes, my son...different. I made one farm; you made three. Your five brothers made one farm each. I married three women; you married just one...we are all different, Kallon. Everybody is different."

"In that case, Tamba is different from me because he is lazy."

"Tamba is not lazy," Galakpai challenged. "He has a different spirit. If he is lazy, no one would go after him...like this American man, who used the word *opportunity*."

"Opportunity. Can Tamba feed his wife and children with opportunity?" Kallon challenged.

Galakpai giggled.

"So you agree with me," Kallon added.

"The American man says Tamba is best at what he does," Galakpai corrected. "Should he not take a chance?"

"A chance at what?"

"I don't know, Kallon, but this stranger is seeing something that the boy has. We are not seeing it because we do not know it. Tamba will be attending school, will he not?"

"What does school have to do with it," Kallon grunted.

"Tamba will become educated, will he not?"

"Educated," Kallon mocked. "I wish my son to succeed me from my cassava farms. That is what I am sure of...not playing ball or attending

---

20   *Someone with authority*
21   *Graduation from traditional male school*

school. Perhaps I am single-minded, but can you blame me? All the university-educated sons from Chakporma finished their school and moved to Monrovia[22]. They all want to live in Montserrado so they build their cement houses there. They should help improve village life and farming techniques...with all their education. Not one of them has come back to put a well in their village, a well...so their old mothers do not have to walk to the streams to get water."

"You are right," Galakpai agreed. "But Tamba has his own spirit. He is different."

"Father, different or not, you molded me into the man I've become. You did not allow me to do as I pleased, you showed me," Kallon insisted. "I don't care what that American man says, I will show my son how he is to grow."

"Are you not going to let him go?" Galakpai asked.

"No," Kallon replied in decided tone.

"I see," Galakpai said. "You've already decided. Just remember that *time* stops for no one."

Kallon looked at his father's face.

"Please, listen to me," Galakpai pleaded. "I did not force you to become a goat herder because of whom you are. I did not encourage you to marry more than one woman. We are not all the same, Kallon, as I've stated. Everyone...when you are born, you are clearly defined... you are given certain spirits or you may call it tools. You are born in a specific place, at a specific time, to specific people and to do a specific job. The strength and knowledge you were born with made you a farmer. That was the energy God gave you. Maybe Tamba has already identified what his job is to be."

"Father, does God give a man the spirit to play instead of the spirit to work? Who takes care of his family while he is playing? It is shameful! Shame has no hold on lazy men and a lazy man is a reflection of his father. I want my son to know me the way I know my father. But talking to my son is like talking to a stone. The stones do not hear you, do they? I am responsible for Tamba. I cannot fail him."

"I am not talking about playing, Kallon. Tamba is going to school to become an educated man. So what if he plays ball while attending school?"

"He does not go to school to learn, Father. Tamba goes to school to play football!"

"He is learning something," Galakpai challenged. "Tamba already knows how to read and write…none of us can."

"That's true," Kallon answered coldly.

A familiar fear came over Kallon and made him laugh. His laughter sounded false. His father, his only ally, was now openly siding with Finda. What did they see that he could not see? Or, why were they not seeing what he is seeing?

"When my father told me things, I listened. I did not ask for explanations," Galakpai baited. "Let your son put his energy to where his spirit is. If God has made it possible for Tamba to use his ability, let him go. Do not be the one to stop it. Since Tamba does not want to follow your footsteps to become a farmer, let's be happy he can get an education to become a leader in our village."

"That's how you see it, Father? When Tamba becomes educated, I hope he remembers to build his cement house here. Rest assured… he will be just like the others."

"He will build his concrete house here," Galakpai touched the ground with his finger. "Right here. Tamba will be the sun for Chakporma…a new beacon of hope for the entire Foya District, not Montserrado…but Lofa."

"Maybe, Father…maybe," Kallon replied wearily.

"You've worked very hard today, Kallon," Galakpai said, looking at his son's face. "You are tired. I am tired."

"Yes, Father, I am very tired," Kallon admitted and got up to leave.

"Tamba will be the one to build his cement house in Chakporma," Galakpai repeated.

"I hope so," Kallon replied. Then added, "A father's advice provides the nourishment that his children need to grow…giving them knowledge from day-to-day…teaching them what they need to know. I've done what I can do. I hope in the end, my three children have all they need and are happy about it."

Galakpai uttered a soft laugh.

"That is how it is," Kallon said.

"Kallon, you are a good father," Galakpai praised his son. Then touching his lips with his finger, as if to think better, he said, "You have supported your family with your lips as well as your life."

Kallon nodded his head for the sake of agreement. He slowly

turned his back and walked off. Kallon would never admit to himself or anyone for that matter, all work and no play had taken the joy of life away. But his world without the modern conveniences of electricity and plumbing was still perfect, western culture is odd here anyway. Even music and dancing did not matter much, farming was his life. He was happy as long as Finda maintained the unchanging menu of torborgee and rice.

Kallon returned to his hut and went straight to his children's room. In lantern flickering light, he checked Kumba first, and made sure her arms and legs were covered with the blanket to protect them from mosquito bites, and then he checked the boys. Tamba had seemingly covered Borbor as they both lie on their bed, snoring. Kallon went to his room and lied down next to his wife, resting his head on a pillow.

Before falling asleep, Kallon thought about what his father told him when he was a young boy, about Borbor's age. Once, he had built a model toy truck out of palm wood and was afraid someone might take it while he was sleeping, a cousin or another child in the village. Galakpai assured him no one would steal it because, 'When the world is sleeping, God holds everyone's life and everything they own in His hand'.

****

The morning light emerged and unveiled Chakporma from its blanket of darkness. The village gradually awakened and people began their daily routine. Kaifa and Ryan arrived when Finda was putting her rice bread in the breadbox. After greeting her, Kaifa ordered four muffins before she had the chance to offer her guests any.

"This is the famous Sawie bread," Kaifa said to Ryan and handed him a muffin. "Taste it, you will see why."

Ryan nibbled on the side of the muffin, as a mouse does; showing some interest in the food. "Mmmm...it's good, what is it," he sang and sank his teeth into it.

"I told you," Kaifa laughed and went right to the business at hand. "Ma Sawie, we've come to see your husband," Kaifa said in the Kissi language.

"There he is," Finda pointed, as Kallon was walking toward the kitchen before going to his farm. "Morning, Kallon," Finda greeted her husband as soon as he entered. Her voice was sugary. "They came back to talk to you," she announced the men's presence.

Kallon smiled, hiding his low spirits. He shook hands with Ryan, then Kaifa. "You are early," he said to Kaifa in Kissi language.

"We wanted to see you before you went to the farm," Kaifa replied in English.

"This American man means business," Kallon said, in Kissi. "Who wakes up this early unless he is going to his farm? Take him to the porch, over there," he pointed to the side of his hut. "I will join you there shortly."

"Ma Sawie, don't let Tamba walk to school today, he will go with us," Kaifa said to Finda. Then he ushered Ryan to the porch.

The morning breeze was enjoyable. Ryan followed Kaifa to the veranda and the men found suitable seating and sat down. Kallon joined them, putting his work on hold. He placed his stool, a low seat made of natural plank, in front of his guest, forming a small circle, intimate enough for serious discussion. Kallon thought to be polite, but not overly so, though harsh words were not to escape his mouth. Soon the rays of the morning sun peered through the worn thatched roof of the veranda to brighten the walls.

"Mr. Sawie, thank you for giving me another chance to discuss my unexpected visit with you. I am sorry if I have disrespected you in any way," Ryan apologized.

Kaifa interpreted.

Kallon nodded. He was one who believed in words more than the face who uttered them.

"Have you seen Tamba play?" Ryan asked Kallon.

Kallon shook his head *no* even before Kaifa interpreted. He had never watched a football game.

"Tamba has a special gift for soccer," Ryan continued "We are forming a football team to take to the Olympics. Have you heard of the Olympics?"

Kaifa interpreted.

Kallon shook his head, no.

Kaifa explained in Kissi language what the Olympic Games were about—an international athletic competition, generally held every four years in a different location, consisting of summer events, like soccer.

"The Liberian government has hired Mr. Muller to assemble a team to represent our country. He thinks Tamba is good enough to play on our team," Kaifa finished proudly.

"They, meaning the Liberian government, want my son to play football?" Kallon sneered.

Kaifa interpreted.

Ryan forced a smile and nodded.

"If we depend on that government, Chakporma will be a village with nothing," Kallon finished. "We simply exist while they are living."

Kallon waited for Kaifa to interpret.

"Mr. Muller, all my life…my father paid hut tax…I, too, have paid…I cannot tell you and my father cannot tell you what our government has done for us. What was that hut tax for? They simply empty our poor pockets to fill theirs."

Kaifa interpreted.

"They don't care that market women suffer the inconvenience of poor roads, no light in the village…no running water…but the government has sent you to ask me to take my son from the farm so that he plays ball like a lazy fool?"

Kaifa interpreted, word for word.

"Oh, no Mr. Sawie, it's not like that," Ryan said, right away. "I am not here on the government's behalf. I am looking out for your son."

Kaifa interpreted.

"In what way," Kallon asked. "Show me."

Ryan processed his thoughts quickly, wondering how best to explain to Mr. Sawie what the opportunities would mean for the man's son. By way of Kaifa's interpretation, Ryan expressed the need to rebuild Liberia, starting with the youth. Being a team member— via inclusion, teamwork and building trust—playing sports will be a crucial role in rebuilding Liberia. The young people will develop their potential and be able to compete at every level internationally.

"Your son has the talent and as long as he is guarded by a coach, he will be ready should an opportunity arise," Ryan said; Kaifa interpreted.

Kallon waited to hear more.

"Competition in football is intense, but opportunities are available," Ryan continued. "Tamba is approaching two roads here…joining Lone Star for the Olympic or joining a major league team someplace else. Either way, I will find a scholarship for him to continue his education while he is playing."

Kaifa interpreted and also explained what a scholarship is.

Kallon's stare softened. "Are you asking me to put my son's life in your hands," he asked.

Ryan heaved a sigh and said, "I am volunteering to take Tamba under my wings, Mr. Sawie…only God can take someone's life in His hand."

Kaifa interpreted.

"Yes, good friend, that is true," Kallon agreed.

"Mr. Sawie, finding a scholarship won't be easy, but I will make sure of it. If Tamba is recruited by a professional team, he wouldn't need a scholarship to attend school, he'll make more than enough money with a good contract. I will make sure Tamba continues his education, whether he's playing for Lone Star or any other team. Every contract we sign, it will have to include him attending some academic institute. I'll make sure of it. That's what I'm promising…I'm giving you my word."

Having an interest in only his guests, Kallon did not see Tamba standing in the doorway until Ryan waved at the boy. He turned and noticed Tamba had tears in his eyes. Kallon heaved a heavy sigh.

"Come to me, my son," Kallon said.

Tamba came forward and stood before his father. He blinked and tears fell from his eyes. Kallon starred at his son's face with a long empathetic gaze.

"If you want to play ball for Mr. Muller, I will not stop you," Kallon proposed, "As long as you work hard at school."

Tamba looked down at Kallon's smiling face and was comforted. Finally, he had the assurance of someone he'd always wanted to please and did not know how.

"I am videotaping all of our trainings and skirmishes from now on," Ryan said. "These videos will be sent to different high school and universities coaches across the United States. When they see the level of Tamba's play, someone will notice his potential."

Kallon smiled after Kaifa interpreted.

"We are playing the final skirmish in Voinjama, the last Saturday next month. I have an idea. Mr. Sawie, would you like to come and see Tamba play?" Ryan asked; Kaifa interpreted.

"All the way in Voinjama," Kallon said, incredulously. "How will I get there? Besides, Mr. Muller, I will be working on my farm. I have to feed my family."

Kaifa interpreted and added, "I will not be there, but the whole of Lofa County might."

"I will pick you up and bring you back after the game," Ryan promised.

The men shook hands on the arrangements.

\*\*\*\*

On game day it was 90 degrees in Voinjama, Lofa County Capital, but everyone was bracing the heat to watch the game. The atmosphere was of expectation because this game was to determine the final picks for the Olympic squad and many people were standing around the entire football field to watch. More people than Kallon Sawie had seen in one place in his entire life. Thankfully, words do not settle soccer matches or final lineup, but final scores do. Of course, the pace and cleverness make the player known for tactical plays.

Soon the players, wearing spanking new jerseys provided by their sponsors—one team in red and the other in navy blue—were warming up on the field. The ref checked his watch and blew the starting whistle. Red team kicked off and the crowd erupted with cheers.

Each side was playing incredible attacking soccer, but Tamba Sawie was blazing fast, dismantling the other team with swift scoring setups. Two minutes into the game Red team won a corner[23] kick. Defenders and offensive players waited anxiously for a chance when the kick was taken. Wearing number seven, Tamba Sawie out-jumped every player in the box[24] and skinned the ball lightly with his head by the stunned goalkeeper—GOAL!!! Red team scored.

"He's like that," Ryan said to Kallon. "Always totally unmarked."

Kallon did not understand what the word 'unmarked' meant, but he saw what his son had managed to do; the goal was quick. He nodded approval.

Red team stayed hungry, pushing forward, at times looking supe-

---

23    *Corner kick is awarded to the team when the ball passes over the defending player's goal line, with a defender having touched the ball last. Corner kick acts as a direct free kick taken from the corner of the field—if the ball passes the line on the left of the goal, the corner is taken from the left corner and if it passes on the right, the corner is taken from the right corner.*

24    *A rectangular box—sometimes called the "penalty box"— 44 yards wide by 18 yards deep. It includes an arc 10 yards from the "penalty mark". Handball and fouls committed in this area may result in a penalty kick (a direct free kick by an offensive player shooting for goal from the penalty spot, which is 11 meters, perpendicularly on goal, with nothing but the goalkeeper to beat).*

rior to Blue team. They moved the ball effortlessly around until they reached the edge of Blue team's box, but took a poor shot. Blue team countered, taking the ball into Red team's box, but it was hastily cleared by Red team's goalkeeper.

Before this match, there was a sense of bemusement that Lone Star could never go as far as the qualifying round among the African teams; although Liberia has always had great players. In fact Liberia had the best African player, FIFA[25] player and European Player in the image of one man, George Weah. While there are other great Liberian players also, it still seemed as if they'd failed to inspire Lone Star to reach the world stage; even as much as five games away from world titles. Success in choosing the right talent for the new Lone Star team could spark real belief, so Ryan thought. They had to start building from somewhere.

When Sawie took the ball at midfield, everyone burst into applause, cheer-clapping, "Deer Boy! Deer Boy!" Some Blue team players were clinical in denying him the ball, let alone a shot, but that rarely happened. Teammates on both teams knew opponents cannot always swarm Tamba Sawie's touch. He is quick as a deer. Watching him play is like watching a pinball game. He is always perfectly placed for every pass. Just twenty-five yards from the box, Sawie fed a charging teammate on his right, dropping the ball off to him rather than taking the shot. The teammate sent it well over the bar[26], wasting the opportunity to extend Red team's lead.

"Good job," Ryan said, clapping his hands a few times, praising Tamba's decision, not the miss.

Not understanding soccer is a team sport, Kallon shook his head, wondering why the boy did not take the shot himself.

The early goal had certainly jump-started the action, the crowd cheered relentlessly while the players settled into midfield with quick skirmishes. Clinically attacking and clinically defending, Red and Blue teams changed momentum. With so much game to be played, time to get comfy was light-years away. Not that it would be possible to get comfy in a match where players are selected for the national team.

It was close to half time and finally Blue team got their best chance,

---

25    *Acronym used for the worldwide soccer association; Federation of International Football Association*
26    *Goal post*

twenty yards on a free kick after one of their players went down. The kicker tried to bend the ball, but the curl was slow and with too much height. A little over forty-five minutes later, the ref whistled the end of the first half.

Tamba ran to his father, "Papa…Papa…did you like it, Papa?"

"Yes…Tamba, yes," Kallon said, smiling. "The ball is your hoe and cutlass. You control it with your foot like I use the hoe with my hand. Tamba, they were calling you a *deer*."

"Papa, that's my football name," Tamba said, beaming. In his mind, he promised to be a lot better in the second half because *Deer Boy* had purposefully held back.

Ryan lectured each team, giving pointers on how individual players were to show their true talents. He wanted strikers to take more shots so that the goalies were tested.

The second half started.

Blue team started with pure determination to equalize. A player made a great turn in the box and almost slotted the ball past the goalie, but the keeper got his hands on it, drawing cheers.

"Good save," Ryan said, praising the goalie.

Kallon could not understand why Ryan was cheering Blue team. "Whose side is he on," he said in Kissi.

Blue team built another attack, as the match continued, and won a corner. Ryan instructed the kicker to try a short one. The eventual cross was punched away and the rebound shot was deflected for another corner. The corner was taken. A Blue team player took a headshot, but the ball went way too high over the goal. Another clear chance to score missed.

Kallon's presence on the sidelines looked to be the match needed to kindle Tamba's true fire. It seemed a perfect moment to give his father reasons to believe in his dream. Tamba decided to get Red team to a 2-0 victory. On account, he would provide fresh plays from his own head, the ones he'd daydreamed of for a long time; alongside bits and pieces of inspirations for his teammates. *Deer Boy*, aka Mr. Clutch had the plot secured for the last five minutes of the game in his head.

Cheers erupted when Blue team goalie saved the team from an extended lead, denying Tamba's first try. Tamba tried once more, but the goalie saved that attempt also. So far Blue team goalie had pulled out many brilliant saves and continued to do so, but Tamba did not wilt. He was now eyeing the clock with his mind's eyes and there was no way he would let his plot head into failure.

As the match went on, there were attacking advantages for both teams and more cohesive counterattacks. Finally, in the 88th minute, number seven found the net and it was effortless and easy. Tamba felt it coming, running parallel and taking the same route as a teammate with the ball on his right. Driving all the way to the end line, the player—with the ball—drew the keeper out and surprisingly dropped the pass to Tamba Sawie. Uncovered, Sawie sweetly tapped it into the net. It was as if God's hand had channeled the whole thing. It was perfect. Cheering and clapping broke out.

"Your son makes the best players look like a week-old soda…flat," Ryan said to Kallon. There was excitement in his voice and Kaifa was not there to interpret it. "Tamba good-o," Ryan said in simple English.

This brought a big smile to Kallon's face. He had watched his first football game and the scoreboard had only Tamba's name on it. He had not realized his son, the lazy one, was a magnificent athlete. This was how Kallon Sawie knew Liberia had a super star football athlete. He counted twenty-two players on the field, but only his son had scored two goals.

The game was beautifully played in art form, like ballet, where it was all style. The score did not matter much, it was the strategies of individual players that were judged and the best players would be selected for Lone Star's future squad. The new Lone Star was not about eleven simple draft horses running up and down the field, it was about building up a strategy and ability, mainly injecting national pride in Liberia's youth. That was Ryan's objective. Nigeria, Africa's other child, had actually won an Olympics gold medal. Liberia could.

"The place God calls you to, is the place where your deep gladness and the world's deep need meet."—**Fredrick Buechner**

*From the writer's pen*

Whatʼs true for one man is true for all—humans are made out of something so ordinary, and that *something* is dust. What makes us extraordinary is God's special ingredient, His very own breath, the breath of life. But like grass withers and flowers fade, our life is brief and seen by few. That makes every person a special person, an extraordinary beauty to say the least.

Each life has a purpose, each life is precious and every life should be treated as such. Humanity flows from within, outward; thus making it possible to touch the lives of others. So, for us to be caregivers, kindness must flow out of our hearts. And so the story goes, in Firestone.

In some sections of the story, everyday Liberian colloquial English is used in the dialogue between some characters. This glossary is provided to help my reader interpret the message of each character. The words in the left column are the pronunciation (accent influenced) for the words in the right column.

| Word | English Word or Meaning |
|------|--------------------------|
| | |
| eh | isn't |
| dey | the or they |
| o and yah | usually the 'o' sound, or yah, is added at the end of a statement to place emphasis |
| any | isn't it not so? |
| tin | thing |
| dis | this |
| ain't | is it not? |
| a | it or is |
| na | not or don't |
| wha | what? |
| gwen | going |
| dem | them |
| looka | look at |
| na | now |
| tank | thanks |

# Firestone

Huber studied the mob at the airport with a frown on his face. "Some vacation," he murmured to himself. School was out, it was close to Christmas and he was in a foul mood. His Mom and Dad had planned this trip for three years, both taking on part-time jobs to earn extra money, just to spend Christmas in Liberia. How far was Liberia from Atlanta? As far as the moon, he thought. Huber overheard his parents say the trip cost close to sixteen thousand dollars. He just didn't get it, why did they want to spend Christmas, of all the days in the year, in a place with no plumbing, no electricity, no cable, no phone and especially no snow. He wasn't sure if Santa got that far and he didn't care. He'd outgrown the *Santa coming down the chimney* crap, anyhow, but still. All his buddies would be in Atlanta having fun and he would be in Africa. What a shame!

"Y'all will have fun," Cecelia promised the children for the hundredth time, staring at them, smiling.

They were following the line, boarding pass in hand, marching down the concourse. They passed by tiny airport shops packed with people and when they passed Santa Claus with the clapping bell, Huber looked at his mom, then his dad, and finally his younger sister. Everyone seemed eager. Mylaeka gazed at Santa, hand clutched in Cecelia's hand and lollipop strapped tightly against her back. She didn't look happy or sad. As long as Mylaeka had everything she cared about in that pink backpack of hers, a bag made in the shape of a poodle she'd named *lollipop*, she was okay.

Before leaving the house, Mylaeka made sure her Amazon Kindle, her iPod and her digital camera were tucked away in lollipop for safe keeping. All her power chargers were packed too. She smiled at the thought of making extra money, knowing Huber would forget to pack his and might need to use hers. Then, she would charge him fifty cents each time. At the end of the family's last vacation, Mylaeka was six dollars richer. Every penny she made came from Huber having the need to charge his gadgets.

Moussa was instructed to pick up Wicky, Cecelia and their two children from Roberts International Airport early Monday morning and drive them to Monrovia, where Wicky's in-laws live. From there, Moussa was to take them to Varney Bah's home in Kakata.

Kakata, the fifth most populated area in Liberia, is the capital of the 13th county, Margibi County. Margibi County was founded in 1984 when two territories, Marshall and Gibi, were removed from Montser-rado County and merged to form Margibi—*Mar* for Marshall Territory and *Gibi* for Gibi District. Firestone, the world's largest rubber plantation,  is in Harbel, Margibi County. The County can boast of two excellent educational institutions; Booker Washington Institute (BWI) and Kakata Rural Teacher Training Institute (KRTTI). Also located in Margibi is Roberts International Airport (RIA), Liberia's only international airport and main gateway to the country.

On their way to Kakata, traffic through downtown was heavy beyond belief. At one point, Moussa was stuck only because of one driver waiting to pull out of a parking space. There is no give and take driving ethic in the city—you go then I go or I'll give you a little room to maneuver so everyone can drive on—nothing that reasonable. A small gap opened and everyone from all sides pushed ahead trying to be first. Traffic came to a complete halt. Surprisingly, there was no road rage, just a big fat traffic jam and deafening car horns.

Traffic got worse and Cecelia regretted coming to Monrovia directly from the airport. Pedestrians were walking all around slow-moving the cars without any regard for the traffic. As Moussa moved forward, people walked in front of the car. It seemed they were inten-tionally blocking the car, or so Mylaeka thought. Then there were young male vendors pushing two-wheel carts operating as if they were the only ones on the streets. Moussa saw a small gap and attempted to make his way forward, but a cart-operator squeezed in the gap, scraping Varney's brand new Toyota Land Cruiser.

"Oh brother!" Huber gasped. "I knew we should have stayed home for Christmas." Huber was not a happy boy, leaving his friends behind.

"It will be okay, Huber," Cecelia assured him, again.

Moussa exchanged words with the cart-operator and the guy came around to the driver window.

"If dey people was not in dey car I was comin whip you," Moussa threatened in thick Liberian accent.

Wicky and Cecelia burst out laughing, understanding Moussa's heavy Liberian accent.

"What did he say," Mylaeka asked and Cecelia explained as best as she could.

"Con try it," the cart-operator challenged.

"Don't let the man disrespect you because of us," Wicky encouraged, knowing Moussa was holding back because of his boss's guests.

The cart-operator daringly reached his hand in the driver's window, intending to hit Moussa. Moussa slapped it away. The retaliation happened rather quickly. Moussa applied the hand-brake, put the car in neutral, undid his seat belt, opened the door and stepped out, in the middle of the traffic jam. One look at the six-foot giant of a man, the cart-operator took off running, abandoning his cart. "He na meet his match," someone yelled and the crowd applauded with laughter. Even Huber laughed, seeing his first action in Liberia. There was excitement in his giggles.

While in Monrovia, Moussa drove them around neighborhoods and through the markets. Huber soon found out that there is a strong American presence in all facets of life in Liberia. For one thing, even though Liberia has its own Liberian Dollar, the American Dollar is also used as a second currency. He noticed boys and men wearing baseball caps with Braves logo and some dressed in Lakers t-shirts and Nike sweats and shoes. A vendor's tray was stockpiled with candies he ate in Atlanta—M&M's, Snickers, Mars bars, Butterfingers, Twix, LifeSavers and Skittles. There were even the same chewing gums too, like Hubba Bubba bubble gum, Juicy Fruit, and Chicklets, his mom's favorite.

From Monrovia to Kakata, Moussa drove very carefully on the road, on account of his passengers. Mylaeka took notes of all the places they passed while driving the Monrovia-Kakata highway; Careysburg, Glita, Cookies Town, where she thought cookies were made. Cecelia corrected her and Huber teased. The children were surprised to see small taxis and pickups packed to triple capacity. Motorcycles (slightly bigger than mopeds) called *Pahn-pahn* traveled on the highway as well. Moussa explained how people use whatever they had access to for transportation. As they drove through small towns, Huber and Mylaeka took pictures of people walking alongside the highway with babies on their mothers' backs and small children ambling along. After about an hour, Moussa turned off the highway, made several left and right turns, and they had finally reached their destination.

The metal gate they were in front of was covered with Christmas lights and a Christmas wreath, as Varney had prepared to meet his children. The large five bedroom house Varney Bah owned was perched on well kept grounds of neat landscape. The walls surrounding it were about seven feet high, topped with jagged chunks of glass and broken glass bottles, to discourage anyone considering climbing over it. After the war, homeowners took extra precautions to keep their families safe.

Varney Bah was happy and anxious to see the son he had not seen for more than twenty years. He told his friends it was the first time he was *laying eyes on his grandchildren*. His son, Wicky, had helped him rebuild his life and was finally bringing his children home to meet their grandfather. Varney was ready to show his son the result of the money he'd sent him from America; a big house and a successful business. Wicky would be proud to see that his father's hard work did not end with the war in 2003.

To claim that one group of people are responsible for the war in Liberia is not fair, but to state that many innocent Liberians lost their lives is accurate. There are always several sides to every story and many roads untaken. Some Liberians worked hard and were successful before the war. Others did not plan to fail, but failed to plan, so life for them was not as successful as they wished.

Varney Bah's workday always started on rooster time (before the sun came up) and he worked hard. But wartime robbed him of his taxi business, his auto repair shop and his wife, who was killed during the war. He was beaten and threatened with execution, but released when one soldier realized that Varney had once been his employer and had taught him to repair cars. Fleeing to Ghana, Varney stayed there for ten years, repairing cars for survival. With financial help from Wicky, he opened a mechanic shop in Accra and with the proceeds, bought two taxis. Gradually, the business gained momentum and he purchased two more. The war left many Liberians severely challenged in meeting their economic needs, but Varney returned to Liberia in 2006 with six new taxis to set up Bah Taxi Service, regaining respect in Margibi County. In five years Varney was able to employ ten full time drivers to run his taxis and four mechanics to work in his two auto repair shops. The skills Varney got from training as an auto mechanic at BWI had made his success possible before and after the war.

BWI—Booker Washington Institute—was founded in 1929 as a school modeled after the Tuskegee Institute in Alabama, USA. Tuskegee was famously first directed by Booker T. Washington, who hired several notable faculty members, including George Washington Carver, renowned in America for his resourceful scientific inventions. Carver published many uses for simple agricultural products grown in the American South. He found, for example, that hundreds of useful products, from dyes to cosmetics to plastics and gasoline substitutes, could be made from peanuts, sweet potatoes, and soybeans.

Like Tuskegee Institute, BWI embraces the educational philosophy of educating the mind and hands—a theoretical and, at the same time, practical concept of learning. The school housed students on campus in dormitories and some students commuted to school from various communities around Kakata. BWI graduated students in agriculture, auto mechanics, business education, building trades, electricity, electronics and home economics. The institute, like other higher institutions of learning in Liberia, was devastated during the war, but is gradually rebuilding.

Varney Bah took his grandson to his auto repair shops and introduced the boy to his employees. The introduction came with the story of how he started many years before the war. While attending BWI, he rebuilt an old car, restoring it to fair condition and ran it as a taxi. With hard work and persistence, Varney was able to save enough money to buy a new one. That business grew into a fleet of six taxis before the war "spoiled" everything.

"I'm sorry, grandpa," Huber said and it brought Varney to tears.

"One day, I want you to return to Liberia and take over Bah Taxi Service, okay?" Varney said to his grandson.

"Will my daddy let me?" Huber asked.

"Of course, he will," Varney said, "Why he will not let you?"

The drivers and mechanics accommodated the boy's visit, showing him how to drive a car and how an oil change is done. One driver actually let Huber drive a car! Something he could never do in America. His vacation was definitely getting better, a whole lot better.

While Huber hung out with Grandpa Varney, Mylaeka spent her time quietly reading books on her Kindle or listening to an audio book or music. Most thought she was shy and being aloof, but the eight-year-old had a passion for words; books and mature conversations. She loved to read. Cecelia hoped spending time in Liberia could change that, especially the way children in Liberia were. They spend all day outdoors playing games together; Na-foot, hopscotch[1], hand-clapping games, zekee-solo-ma[2], games Cecelia remembered playing while growing up in Monrovia.

It wasn't April first, April Fool's Day, but children playing in the neighborhood were singing the April Fool's Day song:

> *April fool*
> *Go to school*
> *Tell your teacher, he's a fool*
> *If he beat you, do not cry*
> *Pack your books and say, 'good-bye'*

"You should go out and make friends with the neighbor's children," Cecelia encouraged Mylaeka. "Let them teach you some of the games I used to play here when I was your age."

Mylaeka preferred reading her Kindle instead. With a little more encouragement, she went outside and made friends with the neighbor's children. However it was on account of their pet monkey, Momo. She'd never seen a real live monkey before and thought it was neat to have one for a pet. Momo was kept on a very long chain tied to the base of a guava tree. He was not like a dog or cat that could be somewhat controlled, but Momo knew a few tricks. He climbed and hung on the tree branches and walked on two feet. Momo also moved

---

1    Game in which a player tosses a small, flat object, as a stone, into one section after another of figure drawn on the ground, hopping from section to section to pick up the object after each toss.
2    Standing opposite, you hop back and forth, clap once and salute with one hand; and let the opposite player, doing the same, salutes also. Guess the same hand and become the leader in the game.

around a lot, left and right, up and down, through and around, being a monkey. Mylaeka asked Cecelia if she could take a pet monkey like Momo with her back to Atlanta, the one her neighbor had promised to bring from up country.

Cecelia's lips couldn't say what her mind was saying, "*Are you nuts! We can't even afford a dog.*" Instead, she said, "Sweetie, have you seen anyone with a pet monkey in Atlanta?"

"No," Mylaeka pouted.

"Well, neither have I," Cecelia said, with a smile to hopefully cheer up her daughter. "We cannot take a monkey to Atlanta, but you can play with Momo as much as you'd like to…until we leave."

Still, Mylaeka didn't smile.

"Why don't you use your camera to take pictures of Momo doing those crazy things you tell me about. Use those pictures and make a PowerPoint presentation for your friends in Atlanta," Cecelia suggested. "I think they will like that."

That did it. Mylaeka's eyes widened and she smiled from ear to ear. "I will, Mommy, I will," she exclaimed and went running to start the project.

Two days in Liberia and Huber already had a different feel for things in Africa. Then it happened, a man was caught breaking into his grandfather's home. No one knew how the thief got on the property or how long he had been there until he'd walked sideways, like a crab, halfway around the house. It was over the slight sound of snoring when the watchman heard the intruder and yelled, "Who da?"

With a sinking heart, the thief realized he was busted and took off running. As if it was an unhurrying chase or an unperturbed pace, his feet grew heavy as he fled from the crowd of about ten men. He could not outrun the strong feet that followed and everyone hollering, "Rogue! Rogue! Rogue!" The mob's untiring pursuit of the thief was pure determination, their undying desire to catch him did not cease. The intruder ran.

The rogue felt the nightstick. It felt as if a shield, a wall or something hard and cold, had slammed into him, icing his strides. His knees buckled and before he knew it, he was on the ground, yelling, curled into a ball so tight no one could get to his hands or feet. A voice had said to him, "Cry!" And, cry he did, pleading loudly for mercy.

"Pull his legs," the watchman instructed two men. "And you two," the nightstick owner continued, "pull his arms when I count to three!"

On three, four strong men pulled hard and straightened the rogue's body, at the same time pulling his torn t-shirt off him.

"Lay him on his stomach," the watchman demanded, pulling the belt out of the loops of his trousers.

The rogue's back being exposed, one man pointed at the marks and exploded, "Da old rogue this!"

Long and narrow strip markings across the young man's back resembled straps. Undeniably, he had been stricken with a strap, no doubt to punish him. The marks indicated he had gotten them by whipping and the lashes he'd received had, no doubt, placed him a step between life and death.

"Please…I beg ya'll, don't beat me," the rogue pleaded tearfully.

His howling seemed annoying, which angered the watchman more. He did not want to wake his boss, Varney Bah, or the visiting relatives from America. The flogging started. The watchman had flogged the young man ten times with his belt when Wicky Bah stopped him.

"Stop this!" Wicky yelled. Judging from the rouge's face, he looked about fourteen or fifteen. "You are not the one this boy has stolen from. Even if you were the one and have a complaint against him, the courts are there…there are officials. You can bring charges against him, but you cannot be both judge and jury."

"This man is a rogue," the watchman justified.

Wicky argued strenuously that the rogue was still a child although he had done a manly thing. The watchman told Wicky he didn't care; they were the ones living in the shadows of the thief's crimes. He thought Wicky, an Americanized Liberian, in fact a stranger, was beguiled by the thief's empty promises which were uttered just to gain his freedom.

Wicky looked at the boy's back and let out a low whistle. "Put him in the pickup," he demanded. "I'm taking him to Duside Hospital."

Obeying orders, the watchman, with the help of two other men, loaded the moaning young man in the back of the pickup. He promised to flog and torture the rogue if he was ever caught again, warning, "Da man going back to Amerikor," meaning Wicky Bah. "If I catch you here again, I will beat you 'til you poo-poo."

Fear tucked deep inside the boy's chest as the pickup bumped along. He had no idea where they were taking him until the pickup stopped in front of the hospital emergency entrance. Wicky ordered the men to carry the rouge in.

"What is the patient's name," the woman at the emergency room admission desk asked, looking at the boy.

The boy said nothing. His shorts and tee were worn to shreds. He smelled as if he had not had a shower or bath in a very long time. There were beads of sweat visible on his upper lip and tears stain down his cheeks.

"What is your name, son?" Wicky asked, in an encouraging voice.

"Firestone," he answered, in a voice slightly above whisper.

"Firestone," the woman said, doubtfully. "As in Firestone Rubber Plantation?"

He nodded shyly.

She let out a soft chuckle. "Don't tell me your last name is Montserrado," she criticized, shaking her head as she wrote the name down.

The boy moaned, still feeling the pain from the licks.

"What's your last name?" Wicky asked.

Firestone remain mute, staring down at the desk.

"What's your last name," Wicky asked again, slightly annoyed. "Look, I'm only trying to help you."

"I don't know," he mumbled.

"You don't have a last name?" Wicky asked.

"No," he whispered, shaking his head.

Wicky looked at the boy, then turned his attention to the woman. "Do you really need a last name?"

She nodded yes.

"Use mine," he said, and spelled Bah for the woman to write it down.

The woman shrugged and did as Wicky suggested.

Wicky followed the boy when the doctor called to see him. Dr. Tweh seemed apprehensive as she applied medicines and bandages to the fresh wounds on Firestone's back. "Is he your son," she ventured. Her gaze went from Firestone's back to Wicky, furrowing her brow, then back to the boy. The boy looked frightened. "Where did he get these marks, if you don't mind me asking."

"Maybe you should ask him," Wicky said, defensively.

"I intend to," Dr. Tweh replied. "Or, maybe you can explain it to Judge Tweh," she threatened, referring to her legendary father, Judge

Samukai Tweh, who presided over the *Heart Men* case in Monrovia.

Wicky smiled. "No need to," he said and explained his encounter with the boy.

Dr. Tweh finished and said to Firestone, "Young man, you really need to think about your life…stop wasting it. You might not be lucky next time."

Wicky paid the cost for the treatment and Firestone was released. Firestone was not free to go because Wicky wanted to know all about him and insisted the boy take him to where he lives. He reluctantly took Wicky to where he actually slept. Home was an empty building with an old rear car seat inside, raggedy with no legs or spring, which allowed the boy to sink to the floor. One look at the pad and Wicky understood why the young man was addicted to crime.

What had brought Firestone to such a life was a mixed race origin of Africa and Asia. He had never belonged to a family like ordinary people. A family where children giggle and adults talk to each other. A family with real people, a proper family, living in houses they called home, with a mother and a father who are there every night and brothers and sisters who tease each other. Firestone fit everyone's preconception nicely. He was an obvious troublemaker, a failure, the uneducated, unemployed product of a one night stand between a "grona girl,"[3] (a woman whose sexual promiscuity places her outside respectable society) and a horny lonely UN Peacekeeper. Taking on the name of his birthplace, Firestone was alone in his world of poverty with no education or skills and certainly not a good position to be in for a young boy.

This kind of poverty is the same in every part of the world; sleeping on the streets, eating whatever you can steal, living by your wits. God forbid if you have no wits, then you die on the streets. Life can be short and death merciful for the poor. Some, very few, have happy endings and of course not without serious struggles. Life is cheap for the poor man living on the streets and it seems like you're worth just about nothing.

Now looking at Firestone with an objective lens, Wicky Bah saw a different young man after following the boy's life story, regardless of how his criminal career had brought him so close to dying under the hands of an angry mob. Had he not intervened, the boy would have

---

3    *Liberian slang for a street woman*

been clobbered by the mob while others watched. He took Firestone home with him, found some beddings and made a sleeping pad for him in the livingroom.

Firestone was happy to sleep on the floor in a decent house rather than on the street or on the old car seat. Exhaustion made sleep easy, lying on the mat, covered from knee to neck. It was morning when he heard a girl's voice and opened his eyes.

"Mommy, there's someone sleeping here on the living room floor," Mylaeka said in a mature voice, both hands on hip.

Cecelia came out of the bedroom and Wicky followed. She drew a deep breath and mouthed a prayer, "Oh Lord, please don't let it be the rogue from last night."

"That's him, honey," Wicky whispered. "I told him he could spend the night here."

"The rogue?" Cecelia gasped. "I thought ya'll took him to the police station last night?"

"Not the police station…the hospital."

"The hospital?"

"Shhhh," Wicky hushed his wife, "Not so loud." Then, he escorted her and Mylaeka to the front porch. "You should see this boy's back, Cecelia," he said, frowning. "He's had so many beatings, I couldn't let the watchman and his men beat him again last night. I don't care if he was stealing."

"I know what you're thinking," Cecelia smirked, studying her husband's eyes.

"I want to help him," Wicky pleaded, before his wife had a chance to say another word. "I just know deep in my heart that's the thing to do…you know, help him."

"But how? We're here for only two weeks."

"He's only fifteen, Cecelia. Did you know the boy was tossed out of the rebel forces when he was ten, never been part of a family before, does not know what happened to his mother after they were separated during the war, has never met his father…I'll be damned if he even knows who his father is," Wicky said in one breath.

He paused.

"Forget school," Wicky continued. "He is too far behind to catch up with his peers. I don't know if he can adjust or much more relate to anyone his age in the civilized world or in a structured environment.

People see him as trouble and for good reasons."

"Are you done?" Cecelia asked.

"Not yet," Wicky said, pointing. "The streets have been his home, he survived on petty theft and has moved on to bigger crimes, breaking and entering into people's homes. Now at that age, between childhood and adulthood, who wants to take a chance on him?"

"Wicky Bah wants to take a chance on him," Cecelia answered. "Is that it," she chuckled. "As always, you ask me the questions I am going to ask you."

Wicky smiled. "That's what my heart is telling me, honey," he whispered.

"You've forgotten we have less than two weeks," she repeated. "And, what if he doesn't want your help?"

"I know he wants my help," Wicky said.

Knowing her husband, Cecelia smiled and left it at that.

Later that day when the police came around for the usual questioning, Wicky informed him there would be no charges brought against the young man. The officer insisted on talking to the rogue, on account that Wicky was the homeowner's son, not the owner of the property broken into.

"Sir, my father is not going to bring charges against his own grandson," Wicky said, convincingly.

"The rogue is Varney Bah's grandson?" The officer said, incredulously, staring with greater interest.

"Well…the young man is my son and I'm Varney Bah's son," Wicky said and handed the officer the hospital's official receipt.

The officer took the piece of paper and studied it. He read to himself the patient's name, Firestone Bah. "You named your son, Firestone, after the people's company?"

"I named my other son, Huber," Wicky said, with a straight face.

The officer smiled. "You Liberians who have become Americans," he chuckled. "Okay, Mr. Bah, since you said Mr. Varney Bah is not going to press charges, I will leave it at that. I'm only doing what your watchman said the old man wanted."

"No charges," Wicky repeated.

The officer nodded and walked away, then out of the gated compound.

Wicky found Firestone sitting on the backdoor steps and sat next to him. He started to ask the boy how he had gotten into the yard with the high fence and jagged broken glass top, but decided not to. He hoped that Firestone would start their conversation and he did.

"When the police come for me, why you no let he take me?" Firestone asked Wicky.

"You knew he was coming, why didn't you run away?" Wicky asked.

Firestone's gaze fell to his feet. Either he didn't have an answer or he didn't know how to answer. For the first time in his life, somebody actually cared about him. The man he had come to rob had carried him to the hospital instead of the police station, he'd fixed him a sleeping pad in the house, fed him food from his own servings and had even given him a good pair of jeans and t-shirt. He did not want to run away when he could have.

"Maybe I didn't turn you in for the same reason you didn't run away," Wicky baited. "Did you want me to turn you in?"

"No," Firestone mumbled. "I wish à was true…dey tin you tell him."

"That I am your father?"

Firestone nodded slightly.

Wicky sighed. "Firestone, if you want someone to be your father, then there are things you'll have to agree to."

The boy's gaze went to Wicky's face.

"Do you understand?" Wicky asked.

Firestone nodded.

"Don't just nod your head, I want to hear it come out of your mouth."

"I muss na steal from you," Firestone muttered.

"I don't want you to steal from anyone, not just me."

"I no go steal 'gain," Firestone promised, "I swear."

Wicky knew the boy was only saying what he thought Wicky wanted to hear.

"It's a hard thing for some people, not to steal, but most people do not steal. Stealing is a bad thing to do, Firestone. You can't take something that is not yours, you just can't."

Firestone looked away, now too ashamed to look at Wicky's face.

"But, you can change," Wicky said. "God wants the rogue to steal no more. Not just me, but God."

Firestone lifted his head and Wicky studied his face. This time,

Firestone did not shrunk in shame at Wicky's staring.

"I tell you what…you can stay with us until our vacation is over, maybe I can help you in some way to change your life," Wicky proposed.

Mylaeka told Huber, (aka sleepyhead) everything she'd overheard and learned about Firestone because he'd slept through the whole incident. Then again, Huber is always the last to know about things while his baby sister is always first. Grandpa Varney told him it was because Mylaeka was an "old soul" in a little girl's body. Huber agreed although he never understood it. The bottom line for Huber was to make the best of his vacation in Liberia. He'd never met a real life criminal before, maybe it would be something he could brag about to his friends when he got back to Atlanta. Huber approached Firestone with intensions of inquiring what life was like without having parents telling you what to do all the time. Bonding between the boys happened on-the-spot.

Firestone told Huber he learned about drinking liquor on his own, by sneaking into bars and drinking unattended drinks. He'd had all kinds of imported beers and Club Beer[4]. He liked Club Beer better because its alcohol content was much stronger. He bragged about knowing what the women drank, Savanna Dry and other wines. Firestone also boasted about the fact he knew every cuss word there is and had actually used them without regret, especially on those who put him down.

"How do you know so much about so much?" Huber asked.

Firestone laughed and said, "Because I live on dey streets."

"Were you scared?"

"Sometimes," he admitted. "But I no let them know I was scare."

"I don't ever want to live on the streets," Huber said and wasted no time warning Firestone about Mylaeka's talent to know everything. "If I did any of these things you did, Mylaeka would tell on me, and I would bet in trouble. I would not want my parents to get mad at me. You don't want Mommy or Daddy to be mad at you, Firestone," Huber warned. "I'm serious."

"Da wha tin dey will do?"

"Punish you!"

"Punish me…but how?"

---

4    *A pale lager beer brewed and bottled in Liberia by Monrovia Breweries Inc—with Swiss Brewers*

"Well," Huber said and stopped.

"Wha?"

"I don't know," Huber admitted. "I just don't do stuff to get them mad at me."

"I na won them to be mad at me," Firestone admitted.

The boys burst out with laughter.

Mylaeka was already giving Cecelia report about their conversation.

"Mylaeka, you have to stop snooping around your brother's business," Cecelia warned. (It was not the first warning).

"Mommy, I try to stop snooping, but it's hard," she whined.

However, in her mind's eye, Cecelia was happy to see her unassigned Secret Service Agent keep up with whatever Huber was up to, especially with Firestone around. Now Mylaeka's snooping seemed imperative. She lightly patted the girl's back, sending her off.

When you are being led to a better place by someone who cares about you, you do not need to fear it. Firestone wanted the changes Wicky expected from him and kept his promises. Even when he was hungry and Kpa, Varney Bah's houseboy[5], refused to give him a portion of the family meal, Firestone did not report it to Wicky. He did not steal food either. Firestone easily climbed fruit trees standing in the yard to fill his belly.

"This tin da something-o," the watchman broke the news to Kpa. "I hear somebody stole dey old man money."

"Firestone got dey money, da ole kuba[6] there," Kpa snarled. "He tin by following the old man son, foot to foot, da it will change him?"

"My man tin he kwi[7] now," the watchman taunted.

They scornfully laughed at Firestone behind his back, of course. Wicky had warned anyone mistreating his son would be dealt with accordingly and promised it would not be on Varney Bah's terms.

It was distressing to say the least, when Varney discovered the money his lead driver had reported for the day was missing, $300 to be exact. The funny thing about it, no money had ever been missing in Varney Bah's house until now. The lead driver normally collected $50 from each driver and dropped the money with his report at the

---

5　　　A man employed to do cleaning or other domestic work.
6　　　Liberian slang for con man / hustler
7　　　Liberian slang for someone citified, as in having the sophisticated style or manner associated with an urban life style.

end of every day. This amount was then paid to the Bah Taxi Service; the driver's pay consisted of whatever was made beyond that.

Varney assembled his employees and invited Wicky to witness his miniature court, on account of Firestone being a suspect. Kpa, the watchman and others were present. Each was asked by Varney, "Did you steal my money?" Each response was a negative, plus speeches along the lines of "the way Mista Varney is good to me, I will never do that to him."

"Nothing like dis happen until dis boy came here," the watchman assured. "I na work for Old Man Varney for more than five years now, I should know."

"Let Old Man Varney bring sassywood[8]," one employee suggested. "I na scared. Dey man who scare to take sassywood is dey person… let dey medicine catch dey person."

"No one is taking sassywood here," Wicky asserted. "You all have accused Firestone of stealing the money, I'll ask him if he did."

"Da ole rogue, Mr. Wicky…you tin he will say he take da money," the watchman challenged.

"Did you see him take it?" Wicky asked.

The watchman said he did not. Everyone was asked and no one admitted seeing Firestone take the money.

Irritation was detected in Wicky's voice. He seemed upset so Varney decided to end things. "Let it be so," he conceded. The discussion stopped momentarily because $300 was not nearly enough to spoil his son's visit home.

Varney turned to Firestone and said, "I don't blame you." He did not say who he blamed, but continued, "If you had come peaceably to me, I could have helped you. I've helped many people, you can ask them," he pointed at Kpa, the watchman and the other employees. "My heart would have easily knit with you. But you came to my place as an enemy. Now, you've betrayed my son so you can steal from me a second time."

"You see what dis one rogue na do here," one employee whispered to another.

---

8    *An ancient practice of trial by ordeal—the accused is exposed to physical dangers, from which he or she is supposed to be divinely protected if innocent. In one kind, a machete is put into a fire. When it gets red hot, the machete is rubbed on the legs of several suspects and the one who gets burnt is declared guilty. In another type, suspects are given a potentially deadly concoction to drink.*

It was out of everybody's hearing, but Wicky heard him clearly and understood the betrayal the man had heard in Varney Bah's voice. Wicky signaled to Firestone to come forward. Stooping, the boy walked cautiously from the group and came to Wicky.

Staring into the boy's eyes, Wicky said, "Firestone, no matter what you tell me, I want it to be the absolute truth. Do not lie to me, you understand?"

Firestone nodded.

"Did you take my father's money?"

Firestone denied it and cried with groaning too deep for words. Wicky left it alone.

Later that evening, Varney spotted his son sitting on the porch and joined him.

"This boy you are trying to help continues to find things before they are missing," Varney complained. "How are you going to manage him from America while he is here? Besides, Wicky, I cannot keep the boy here with me. He's nothing but trouble; he steals."

Varney Bah was expressing his reasons for not allowing Firestone to stay with them when Wicky and his family would return to Atlanta. Although Wicky suggested he would support Firestone from America while he lived at the house. This seemed the most reasonable immediate help Wicky could offer, so he thought.

Wicky said the words without thinking, "Then, I will take him with us."

"Hummf," Varney grasped, "Cecelia will let you?"

"I will talk to her, Pops...my wife is reasonable. We will decide this together."

Varney grunted and said, "You are willing to take a chance on someone who can be a negative influence on your own son. Huber can learn these things from him. Are you not concerned about that?"

Wicky said, "No, Pops, I'm not concerned about Huber. Let me point something out to you, people are not born rogues, situations force them into a life of crime. This young man is a fine example. Before the war, young people in Liberia had a chance to prepare for their future. Remember Teen Time Quiz[9]? Young people had the opportunity to challenge each other intellectually. Educational oppor-

---

9     A question-and-answer game show where Liberian high school scholars matched wits with each other

tunities were there, everyone who attended BWI and graduated, did so with quality training that was reflected in their job performance. Look at us, Pops. What we've learned, coming out of high school, has sustained us and others. We've earned our living. What chance did those poor children have during or after the war?"

Varney Bah looked at his son with confusion.

"Huber's life started differently than Firestone's. Every day I try to steer my son in the right direction and pray to God that he follows. You know, like you did for me. I can't force Huber to follow, he has to see his opportunities and take advantage of them. The way I did. I will try to do the same for Firestone. By now, Firestone should understand something about consequences. He knows what it's like to live the life of a criminal so he will welcome the change. That's what I'm banking on."

"A leopard never changes its spots," Varney warned.

"You know something, Pops, if you are expressing tangible concern for Firestone, it's okay. Be critical of his errors, but you should also praise his progress," Wicky challenged. "Weren't you the same person who taught me correction does much, but encouragement does more?"

Varney kept his peace and Wicky walked away.

The unwillingness of his father didn't bother Wicky at all. It was his decision on which Firestone's life depended for change. The matter had kept him up most nights since the break-in and his vacation had turned into what Cecelia had labeled a rescue mission. She'd said it with a giggle and not a hint of objection.

Cecelia was her husband's partner in every way, since their meeting in high school. All of their decisions were made together (with reasoning of course). After graduating from BWI, Wicky found his way to America and Cecelia joined him one year later. Finding jobs and a place to stay while they attended college—Wicky at Georgia Tech[10] and Cecelia at Georgia State University—was a struggle and the difficulties of life were oppressive. God doesn't promise that believers will escape the turbulent seas of life, but He has promised never to leave nor forsake them. Cecelia remembered that promise. One Sunday she encouraged Wicky to visit a church with her because a voice had told her to. They met Pastor Huber. With the help of Pastor Joseph P. Huber, a white Southern Baptist minister with blindness to race or

---

10    *Georgia Institute of Technology*

national origin, they were able to finish college with money collected from church members and odd jobs.

During dinner, Wicky and Cecelia discussed Firestone's needs and exchanged ideas between sips and bites. Cecelia had some reservations, like exposing their children so close to someone with behavioral problems; the same concerns their grandfather has. Also, they harbored concerns about how quickly the boy would be able to adjust, especially in Atlanta. School was not an issue, they would home-school him, but, how would people outside their home treat him?

"Cecelia, our view of people determines how we treat them," Wicky said. "Those who see Firestone as a loser will treat him with contempt. Those who see him as a lost boy will treat him with compassion. Who do you see when you look at him, a loser or a lost child?"

"Wicky…."

"No, answer me, honey. Who do you see?"

"A troubled child," Cecelia answered.

"Not a troubled child, Cecelia, but a lost boy who wants to belong somewhere."

Cecelia smiled, accepting her husband's philosophy.

Wicky and Cecelia discussed the challenges, pros and cons, of their commitment to helping the young man. At eight-years-old, Firestone was already an adult, learning to survive on the streets, while other children his age were preparing for adulthood. They were in school learning and getting ready for high school. Outside of school, they were spending time with peers and learning socialization skills to get along with people. In high school, they learned relational skills needed for future career. Living in homes with fathers and mothers, even in single-parent homes, children prepared for future family life. Getting ready for life takes work, and Firestone had none of the preparations he needed. How was he expected to get ready for life, now at the tender influential age of fifteen?

Finally, Wicky and Cecelia Bah based their decision on the concept of Christian social obligations, the same one Pastor Huber and his church members used when he gave them a place to stay while they worked to pay for college. Wicky used that opportunity to become an IT (information technology) specialist and Cecelia, a registered nurse.

With time running out, Wicky hired a taxi from Bah Taxi Service for a trip to Monrovia. There was important business to attend to, documents for Firestone from both American and Liberian governmental offices. Wicky spent three days in Monrovia, going back and forth, leaving Kakata very early in the morning and returning very late at night. Varney's heart was heavy, his son he had not seen for more than twenty years was spending too much of his time away from Kakata. He complained to his friends but the palava[11] reached his daughter-in-law, Cecelia, by way of the watchman, who begged Cecelia to think of one thing for her husband to do to satisfy his father so "his heart can lay down". (That's how the watchman had put it).

On Cecelia's suggestion, Wicky planned an outing for him and Varney to take the boys to Nancy B. Doe Stadium to watch a football[12] match. The Invincible Eleven, (IE) was playing Mighty Barrolle in a friendly match. Varney understood Wicky would not leave Firestone behind, so he did not show a hint of disapproval of the boy tagging along. Still, it was obvious he avoided any contact with the boy. And, Firestone could not enjoy the game on account of being accused of stealing Varney's money. Huber thought it was an exciting game, although it ended with each team scoring two goals.

\*\*\*\*

Christmas is the most celebrated holiday in Liberia and the season changes the complexion of the whole country. Everyone comes into the grip of the festivities and celebration.

Varney Bah knew important people and not-so-important people in Margibi, on account of his generosity in the communities. Everybody knew about his son visiting from America and those who could, came bearing gifts. Some in the form of art, but mostly edible goods. Wicky and Cecelia received many things, from batik fabrics, painting and carvings to tropical fruits of all kinds and edible roots, cassava and eddo. Some even offered small farm animals.

On Christmas Eve, the old man next door came into the house from the back door by way of the kitchen. "I bring dis for Oldman[13] Varney son and his wife," he said, holding a squawking hen under his arm. "Where dey people?"

Kpa waved his hand toward the living room, not paying much

---

11    complaint
12    soccer
13    Oldman is used as an informal address or courtesy title for a man of eminent status.

attention. The old man started toward the living room when he stopped him, "Where you gwen wit da?"

"I want give dem dey chicken," the old man said.

Kpa put down the pot he was cleaning and walked to where the old man was standing.

"I brought them dey chicken for their Christmas," the old man explained. He had cane-juice[14] and peppermint on his breath.

Kpa said, "Leave dey chicken here." It was more of an order than a suggestion. "And, you…wait here," he added.

The old man put the hen down, literally following orders. As soon as he did, the hen lifted its tail feathers and deposited a neat little greenish pile on the kitchen shiny floor.

"Looka dey tin you na do," Kpa protested. "Take dey chicken and go outside!"

The old man was not quick enough. Five minutes later, after an exhausting squawking chase, the kitchen floor was covered with loose feathers and chicken poop.

****

At dawn on Christmas morning, Huber was awakened by the distant bleating of the goat in the back yard. The wavering cry puzzled him, thinking someone was stealing their pet. On the day that one of his grandfather's friends delivered the goat, he assumed the goat was their pet, although no one said it was. Different people continued to bring different things and Huber didn't mind owning a goat. He had never seen a live goat before. He counted on the fact that if Mylaeka can talk Cecelia into owning a pet monkey, maybe he could own a pet goat. He did question the possibility of taking both pets to Atlanta on a plane. However, the bleating stopped and Huber felt at ease. After all, the watchman was good at catching rogues.

Wicky woke up and went into the boys' room. Huber wasted no time in telling him what he had heard and wanted to know if the goat was still tied to the post.

"Maybe the goat ran away, son," Wicky lied. He did not have the heart to tell the boy the goat was slaughtered for the Christmas festivities. Sometimes a little fib solved a problem better than the truth ever could. "We couldn't take it with us to Atlanta anyway."

14    *Liquor or gin distilled from sugar cane*

Huber accepted Wicky's answer to be reasonable. (Mylaeka would have probed further). Wicky secretly thanked God in his heart, he was dealing with his son and not his daughter.

"Where is Firestone?" Wicky asked.

"I asked him to find the goat," Huber shrugged.

Wicky nodded and knew exactly where to find the boy.

Happiness was a brand new emotion for Firestone, but it was short-lived; now that he had been accused of stealing. He'd been helpful around the house regardless of the ill-treatment by Kpa, the watchman and others. None of them wanted him there, not even Varney Bah. The boy thought of running away, but wanted to prove his innocence before doing so.

Staying out of sight, Firestone sat under the coconut tree with his back against it, staring in the distance in deep thought. He heard light footsteps, then came Wicky's voice, "Firestone."

Wicky handed him a package wrapped with Christmas colors and a white bow. "This is for you, young man…Merry Christmas."

"For me?" Firestone questioned.

Wicky said, "Open it."

He opened the package. There was a brand new shirt, a tie, and a pair of socks. "It for me?"

When Wicky told him it certainly was and there was a pair of gray color trousers with matching jacket and shoes that went with it in the house, a big grin splattered Firestone's face.

"You better go and try it on to make sure it fits," Wicky said, tousling the boy's hair.

"Tank you…," Firestone said, and his voice trailed off.

"Daddy," Wicky finished. "You can call me *Daddy* too, Firestone. Mylaeka wanted to know what you should call me."

"Tank you…Daddy," Firestone stuttered and took off running. He wasn't sure if Wicky heard him. He wished he did and hoped it had not sound strange to Wickly because it sounded strange in his own ears.

The children opened their presents, exclaiming loudly. Mylaeka got the video camera she wanted, Huber got an updated model of the iPod with more storage space. The suit fit Firestone as if it was tailored specifically for him. It was Wicky's suit that he had a local tailor altered to fit the boy, based only on Firestone's physical description to keep it a surprise.

****

They came by foot, taxi and private cars to Varney Bah's compound. The yard and house was packed with friends and relatives, dressed to kill, in coat suits, lappa suits, fashionable dresses with high-heeled shoes; all to have a great time. Varney planned for his guests to enjoy themselves with beer, wines—local palm wine—stout, power rum, soft drinks and plenty of food. It was a celebration not only for Christmas, but also because of Wicky and his family's return to Liberia.

Entertainment was at its best and different groups of cultural artists made appearances. The Liberian Sanny Klor[15] was there with his entourage of musicians. Custom dressed with sequin trimmings down the side of his pants and a long-sleeved shirt, gloves covering his hands and a pleasant mask. His musicians were geared with drums, carpenter's saws, empty beer bottles and old wooden washboards. While the drummers beat intricate rhythms on the drums, musicians sang, stroke a knife against the thin blade of the saw, and ran a spoon up and down the washboard, making a complex musical medley. Sanny Klor danced and performed all sorts of acrobatic tricks to the rhythm, flipping his legs over his head and scurrying around like a crab. People were in awe of his dynamic moves. The guests tipped them nickels, dimes, quarters and dollars for their magnificent performances.

Oldman Beggar was also there. Like Sanny Klor, Oldman Beggar was dressed in a costume, mostly made of rags and his mask looked more comical. While Sanny Klor is skinny, Oldman Beggar is as jolly as the American Santa. He had come with a much smaller entourage, two men. One played the drum while the other tapped on an old bottle. As his name pertains, he had come to beg. While his two musicians sang their song:

> *Oldman Beggar! John the Beggar!*
> *Beg for money, John the Beggar!*
> *Beg for five cents; John the Beggar!*
> *Beg for ten cents; John the Beggar!*

Oldman Beggar playfully wobbled his potbelly and comically fell to the ground, as part of his routine. Everyone laughed. A story was told at the end of his dance. The drummer, who is also the spokesman,

---

15    Santa Claus

narrated a tale of Oldman Beggar's misfortune trip. "While carrying a canoe full of toys," he told the audience, "it capsized and Oldman Beggar lost all of the children's gifts for Christmas, along with his personal belongings."

Sadden by the story, Mylaeka was moved to tears. But Cecelia convinced her that the story was not real, it was just a part of their routine. Mylaeka loved Oldman Beggar more than all the performers, because he resembled the Santa she saw at the airport in Atlanta.

Other culture artists toured Varney Bah's compound; the Snake-baby dancers[16] and the "devils"[17].

One "devil" was 16 feet tall, standing on stilts completely covered with raffia material. They called him, the Tall Devil. He was amazingly agile, effortlessly walking and dancing. Another called a Gbatu, short in size and covered with straw-like materials, incredibly changed his height from three feet to eight feet while dancing.

Mylaeka thought he looked like a hut and asked, "Mommy, why is the hut moving?"

"That's not a hut, honey, that's a performer, honey," Cecelia corrected.

The snake baby dancers were dressed in grass skirts and their bodies artfully painted with white chalk in beautiful designs. They did spectacular flips. Flexible and energetic, they performed skills world class gymnasts perform, tumbling and landing flawlessly. A very young performer, perhaps only five-years-old, landed on the arm of their master with just one leg. In one performance, a dancer balanced her midsection on a pointed knife held under her suspended body. Miraculously, there was no sight of blood when she landed on the blade.

"Awesome!" Mylaeka exclaimed, videotaping every moment of the show.

When Cecelia asked Huber if he was having a good time, he told her, smiling from ear to ear, it was like having a Broadway show in Grandpa Varney's back yard.

"Not a Broadway show, Huber," Mylaeka challenged, "the circus!"

Huber responded, "Whatever."

---

16    *Acrobatic performers / dancers, mainly girls, between ages 5 and 15.*
17    *African-masked dancers; for entertainment or ritual performance. These devils are not to be confused with the western concept of the devil, Satan or demon.*

There they were with Varney Bah on Christmas Day, from morning to past midnight; eating, drinking, dancing and enjoying the performances. It was a joyous feast in the Bah compound, and their host had prepared well.

After Christmas, everybody was still chatting about the missing money and how it had turned Varney into a sour man. They could tell from his face, the watchman pointed out to Wicky.

"You see Mista Wicky," the watchman said, "Dey tin…a strange here. Something like dis ain't happen until da boy got here in dey compound."

"I know it's not Firestone," Wicky replied. "Whatever the person who took the money is up to, we shall see; and very soon, too."

The watchman furrowed his brow and plunged into silence.

****

Amazingly, today's improved technology enables a rookie photographer to create professional looking shots. Mylaeka Bah is no rookie when it comes to using a camera, not even the Sony Handycam she got for Christmas. Somehow, the smart eight-year-old always came up with solutions and this time was no different.

A picture is worth a thousand words, but a video can say plenty, as Varney's houseboy learned that day. What is more embarrassing than getting caught by a little girl when you least expect it? When someone testifies against you, it's one thing; when you are caught in the act that is a another story. It happened this way.

Mylaeka did not put down her new Handycam since she got it Christmas morning and Wicky was anxious to see footage of the performers, especially the snake baby dancers. Impressed with his daughter's eye for near perfect shots, he continued viewing recordings taken days after Christmas. Then he saw it, a taping of Kpa and another man, sitting in the back yard chatting. They were talking in the Bassa language, which Wicky understood. The video revealed Kpa telling his friend how he'd tried to frame Firestone and had not been successful so far.

"When the driver brought the money that day, I took it and hid it. Everyone thinks it is Firestone…even the old man blamed him. But his son likes this rogue too much, so he wouldn't let the old man put him out. I hate that boy. I've been working for the old man and nobody feels I should be the one the old man son likes. I was going to put the money back after Mr. Wicky went back to the States, without that rouge, of course," Kpa said in well spoken Bassa.

Wicky immediately showed the video to his father and Varney Bah sent for his houseboy.

As soon as Kpa came, Varney said, "If this thing hurts you, it is because I have to say it to get it out of my heart. It is about my money."

Kpa broke out into a cold sweat, seeing only he had been called. He stood nervously, casting rapid glances at Varney and Wicky. "Da who lied on me?" he said, and let out a nervous giggle.

"Da yourself," Varney accused, and then showed him the video.

Wicky asked in Bassa language, "Isn't that you in the video?"

Kpa did not know which was more shocking, seeing him in the video or hearing Wicky speak the Bassa language.

"Do you think anyone growing up in Kakata will not be able to speak Kpelle or Bassa?" Wicky asked in Bassa.

The interrogation ended as quickly as it had started; Kpa confessed. Then with Varney's permission, he ran and got the money. Kpa handed the money to Varney and pleaded for forgiveness.

The exposure made Varney's heart sore toward his houseboy. Until now, he had always believed his houseboy's service was done with honor and integrity. Kpa had been cunning, deceptive and sly. Now he is seen as a double-minded man, unstable in all his ways, cleaver in his tricks, enough to swallow Varney's wit in his lies. Had it not been for Mylaeka, he would have gotten away with it.

"I have tried to be good to you people and ya'll know this," Varney said. "Ask everybody here, and at the garage. What I do for you, many are not doing for their own relatives, much more their employees. I would have not known this thing if my granddaughter had not captured it with the camera. The sassywood you wanted did not catch you, it is the  white's man medicine[18] that caught you."

"We are all responsible for the war in Liberia," Wicky challenged, in English, when Varney was finished.

Kpa and Varney frowned, on account of their disagreement. In their mind's eye, they were never in control of whatever that went on in the Liberian government. The war was blamed on people in charge, not them, period.

---

18    *Medicine = magical practices*

"I say it because it is the truth," Wicky continued. "No one in Liberia cared about anyone other than himself. We allowed our country to be destroyed because we were all selfish. No one was willing to do something as long as someone else will benefit from it. Until that changes, nothing in Liberia will change for the good benefit of the Liberian people, and I mean, every Liberian citizen. Thank God, many of us have learned that when you do good for someone, it makes a positive difference for everyone else, not just that one person you are doing good for."

Varney considered the logic and nodded in agreement.

"There's only one step from hate to envy, Kpa, and I think you have taken it," Wicky continued, this time speaking Bassa. "Sometimes we ought to ask God to show us any way we are hurting or hindering others. We can also ask God to help us show love…not man and woman love, but to show others consideration."

The houseboy's gaze fell to the floor.

"Let me show you what I'm talking about," Wicky said. "It is the way you treat people, you must not be jealous of others or boast, you must not be arrogant or rude, you must never be happy when you see wrongdoing, speak against it. You must not do good only to be recognized. Even when no one praises you for doing good, it is okay because  God sees it. We should do good simply to be doing something for somebody, without expecting something in return. Do you think Liberia would have experienced war if we all had treated each other like that?"

"No," Kpa answered in Bassa.

"No one has ever shown Firestone love, so life has been more difficult for him," Wicky continued in English. "To steal is not good, but if I do not help him, he will continue to steal. Firestone did bad things because no one has ever shown him how to be good. He is not a bad person. He is still a child so he can learn to do better things."

"That's true," Varney added, but without much conviction.

"Kpa, you've done a bad thing too, does that make you a bad person?" Wicky asked.

Kpa looked at Varney, then Wicky. "I'm not a bad person, Mista Wicky," he mumbled in Bassa.

"But, you did something that is bad," Wicky said in English.

Kpa nodded.

"Firestone knows you were the one trying to set him up, ask for forgiveness...I'm sure he'll forgive you."

Kpa sighed and rubbed his face nervously.

"I've asked my father not to fire you," Wicky added.

Kpa immediately lowered himself and touched Wicky's shoes, a gesture of sorrow, regret and apology.

"I only hope you've learned something from this, Kpa," Wicky said. "It is possible to be helpful to others even if you do not have money. It is not the money that does the good; it is the deeds. Money can never fill an empty heart, only love can. So, do good when no one is there to see it. This is all I have to say," Wicky finished and touched Kpa's back to accept his apology.

Kpa got up, walked to where Varney was sitting and held his shoes. "I hold your foot[19], Old Man Bah," he begged. "I no want steal from you. Da dey tin I do to frame dey boy. I'm sorry-o."

"Kpa, to know that your hand was in it, this thing has hurt my heart," Varney chided. "I've promised my son that I will not fire you, otherwise I would have. From now on, my eyes and ears will be on you."

"Yeah, Sir," Kpa said quickly.

"Go from my face," Varney ordered, disrespectfully.

Kpa rose and hurried away.

"I have some good news," Varney said to Wicky. "I sent Moussa to Monrovia to pick up the papers for you...they are all here." Varney handed Wicky the big brown mailer.

Wicky opened the envelope, pulled out the documents and sighed. His eyes widened as he read each piece of paper. Every document he needed to take Firestone to America was there, including the boy's passport. Wicky had taken Firestone to Monrovia to process the documents over a week ago. But getting things done quickly at any government run office is slow and they were running out of time. Cutting through all the red tape he could, Varney was able to speed things up.

"Thank you, Pops," Wicky said, grateful. He understood bureaucratic rules and procedures.

"Tomorrow morning Moussa will take you to the American embassy to get his visa...that, I couldn't help you with," Varney said.

---

19    *Liberian slang—to hold one's foot is a gesture to humble yourself in asking for forgiveness.*

"Pops…you've done the hardest part, getting these papers."

Firestone smiled a bright and beautiful smile, after hearing the wonderful news. It was as if he understood fate had finally come calling for him. How wonderful fate can be sometimes, especially when it favors you. His criminal life had led him to his new family. These strangers had treated him like no human had ever treated him before.

The next day, Wicky and Cecelia saw Mylaeka setting up her camera in the kitchen and laughed smugly.

****

Finally, it was New Year's Eve, the mark of one year ending and a new one beginning, both of which are worth celebrating. Resolutions are usually made—that no one has ever kept. It is the biggest party night of the year for some, but for others, it is an opportunity for reflection, gratitude, and transformation or both. For the Bah family, it was the latter. Varney invited his watchman, his houseboy and other employees to join his family while they attended the New Year's watch keeping church service.

"Put on your Christmas clothes," Varney suggested when he gave his verbal invitation.

Service started around 10 p.m. as everyone was dressed in their Sunday best. The message from Pastor Nuquay was about life involvements in the dynamic relationship of moments, where divine energy was opening doors to new possibilities. Moments in which God's vision awakens people to holy endeavors of helping others.

"Amid the change, the reality is we cannot step in the same place twice," Pastor Nuquay preached. "God's mercy is new every morning, so we are to keep watch for divine movements in ordinary time."

The assembly shouted, "Amen!"

"Today, Liberia has more hope than fear," Pastor Nuquay continued. "The Liberian people are still wrestling with unemployment, not enough educational skills and ongoing political gridlock. But each of us can do our part. If we accept the unmistakable biblical call to care for the least of those among us, God will bless us all."

Pastor Topy Nuquay noted the many ways to help others, what New Year's is all about; the quest for new behaviors, new attitudes and new visions to mirror good deeds and hard work.

"We must know how to love…if you have the world's goods and

see your brother in need, don't close your heart on him. That is not love. Let us not love in word or talk, but in deed and truth. God is greater than our hearts and He knows everything!"

The assembly shouted, "Amen-o…Amen!"

"New Year's resolutions, even when they last only a few days, should remind us that we can be transformed," Pastor Nuquay continued. "We should see our lives in a new way. The impact of past and present need not imprison you…you have the choice to shape your attitudes. First, and then your behavior. Remember to treat others with love and care. We may not be related by blood, but everyone is unique and everyone should matter. As you start the New Year, welcome that change…God is doing a new thing for you!"

After singing, praying and giving testimonies, the service ended at midnight. People hugged each other, wishing each other a happy New Year. Many shed tears, seeing relatives and friends in the flesh, while they remembered those lost during the war.

Two days after New Year, the Bah family vacation had run its course. Seeing the desire of Firestone wanting a better life, Wicky and Cecelia Bah's duty from now on was to urge him along toward better achievements in his life. They had every legal document they needed to claim him.

"We came to Liberia with two children, we are leaving with three," Cecelia said, smiling. "A fifteen year old, a twelve year old and an eight year old. Wicky, it's them against us."

"Lord, help us," Wicky chuckled. Then he took his wife's hand and they were silent in their own thoughts. He let go of her hand and pulled her into a tight embrace. "Thank you, Cecelia, for putting up with me."

"We make a good team, honey, don't we," Cecelia whispered. "I love you, Wicky Bah."

The children were watching, waiting to find out why their parents were celebrating. For once, Mylaeka did not have the slightest idea.

"Tell the children," Cecelia suggested. "I can see suspense on my child's face and it is killing her."

"The documents are all here!" Wicky announced, holding up the papers.

All three children ran and surrounded him.

"I didn't know the correct day you were born, Firestone, so I chose December 25th. It was the first day you called me, Daddy. I hope you don't mind."

"I na mind," Firestone said, smiling.

"Is Christmas and your birthday on the same day," Mylaeka exclaimed. There was a hint of envy in her voice.

"Yes!" Huber and Firestone cheered.

****

It takes a minute to say hello and forever to say good-bye. That's because saying goodbye isn't the hard part, it's what you leave behind that's tough. People began gathering at the house to say good-bye and Wicky could tell by the sour look on his father's face that he would miss them. Being strong sometimes means being able to let go and Varney had had to let go of his son many times. However, whenever Wicky left him, his son was always in his heart. Varney hoped the next hello would come sooner than in the past.

"It is a big thing you are doing for Firestone," the old man who brought the chicken on Christmas Eve said to Wicky in Bassa. "It feels good to belong to somebody." Then in simple English he said, "I tank you for him-o." He switched back to Bassa and said, "They say those who have the same destination meet on the same path. Nobody saw this boy as somebody."

"He's somebody," Wicky answered in simple English. "Eh that God made him?"

The old man smiled.

Wicky handed the old man a bottle of cane juice and ten US dollars.

"God bless you-o," the old man said, folding his cash. He stuffed it in his trouser pocket. Then, he held the liquor bottle to eye level and saw not a drop had left it. He unscrewed the cap, tilted his head back and threw the cane juice down his throat. After swallowing he said, "God bless you-o, mista Wicky…ya'll go good[20], yah." He gave the bottle another look, as a man madly in love, smiled at Wicky and moseyed away.

A constant stream of happy faces stopped by the Bah compound to bid farewell to Wicky and his family until it was time to leave. The children hugged Grandpa Varney good-bye and were sitting in the car, waiting for Wicky to join them.

---

20    *Liberian slang when wishing a traveler a pleasant journey*

"Thank you, Pops, for making it happen," Wicky said, shaking his father's hand. This was after their bear hug.

"I realized you were not going to leave without him," Varney said. "God will bless you, my son."

"I couldn't leave without him...and Pops, the only thing on my mind was doing something for the kid. When you decide to help someone, you don't just stop the bleeding...you make sure that the wound has healed."

"I see," Varney said. "You are a good man, Wicky, I wish that there were a few of us and more of you."

"You've done your part, Pops. Look at all these people you're helping here in Kakata."

"Well, God put it on my heart."

Wicky said, "I understand that feeling."

"Yes, you do," Varney agreed. "They are waiting for you, Wicky, you don't want to miss your flight. Ya'll go good, yah."

"Bye, Pops," Wicky said and thought to let Varney know the children had a great time. "Huber, who did not want to spend Christmas in Africa, is asking if we're coming back for Christmas next year. Cecelia and I had a good time too and we are grateful."

"So, ya'll coming for Christmas," Varney baited.

"Who can afford it," Wicky said, furrowing his brow. "I think I've caused my wife enough headaches."

"I will help," Varney offered.

Wicky shrugged. He'd have to run that by Cecelia, but first, she'd better be in the perfect mood for it. Wicky joined his family, but he did not mention what he and Varney had discussed, and the Toyota Land Cruiser rode out of Kakata toward Montserrado County.

*From the writer's pen*

The song, *Sweet Mother*, is one of the most popular highlife songs within Africa. It was released in 1976 by Prince Nico Mbarga (originally from Cameroon but recorded in Nigeria) and his band Rocafil Jazz. The song is a celebration of motherhood, which is the inspiration behind the title of my story. However, this piece of work is simply a tale about nurturance and hope (desire accompanied by chance).

No human has absolute power to turn his or her life around without help, especially God's help, whether you believe in God or not. Believers lean on God's hope. What in heaven or on earth could be too powerful or too much trouble for its Maker? But don't expect God's plan to move with your calendar. Sometimes it is not God's plan for things to move in great haste or move at all. Some things take time, God's time. When you seek God's help, you must learn to accept His timing—a timetable that may move slowly, but it does move for sure.

**Note**[1]


"He is no fool who gives what he cannot keep to gain what he cannot lose."—**Jim Elliot**

---

1    *Information on metastasized melanoma cancer and treatment is meant to give the story creative life; it is not meant to be educational or substituted for medical advice. I encourage my readers to please consult with your health care professional for any medical concern and information.*

## Sweet Mother

The civil war in Liberia left more victims alive than those that died in it. Sundaymah Boye had no one from that past anymore. She did not know what to do to find peace again or how to inject meaning back into her life. It was as if every time God blessed her, she lost it all. She began to wonder that maybe the blessings were taken away because insignificant gods were jealous of her—the lesser gods, that is. Now, the weight of the world had all shifted to her little shoulders and troubles poured like rain. Most times she was unable to hold on to her faith giving her many reasons to doubt even the existence of heaven. But Sundaymah continued to pray daily to God. Little did she know that it was not up to her, but up to God to save her.

Some may say God came in the form of an old woman named Lousue Kai, who had taken on the responsibility of caring for Sundaymah when the ECOWAS soldiers rescued a battered group of civilians in Bassa Community one day. Ma Lousue, as she was commonly known, was a gentle, quiet old woman who sought no recognition and left all the care of her life to God. Others may say God also came as a foreigner, Nick Anderson, an African-American man with unexplained kindness. It seemed the path that Sundaymah had taken was already ordered by God. Little did she know that no matter what, troubles were not going to prevail. She wasn't going to fall because God had prepared the way.

\*\*\*\*

It seemed Sundaymah's beautiful almond colored eyes were made just for crying because that was what they were used for most of the time. She cried because of many things though. She cried when she was happy and when she was unhappy. When she was neither happy nor sad, she cried. She cried about those things she could not feel, things that brought her happiness or unhappiness. She had become a human with a dead soul, like the grave of the child killed to save her life during the war. Sundaymah had cried so much one day Ma Lousue told her, "The way you are crying, the only thing comforting I can say to you is that one day you will stop crying." Sundaymah waited for that day. Eventually she stopped crying. Her tears had become useless because she'd only drown her heart in them.

The day the old woman found Sundaymah was one of those ordinary days that leave no mark on time, holidays like Christmas Day or New Year's or 26th[1] do. Sundaymah thought she had been dreaming, but it was not a dream or maybe it was. One evening as she dozed off, a commanding voice urged her to walk away from her captors—"Just walk," the silent voice commanded. The thought was quite wild, as she was aware that those soldiers had no regard for human life. Rising very early the next morning, while it was still dark, she left the house while her jailers were sleeping. For an unknown reason, they'd forgotten to tie her to the bed. But the war had desensitized Sundaymah so she did not see it as an opportunity to escape. She was driven by a need for a quiet place to calm her broken spirit, a place where only God would get her full attention. In a world like hers, you only wait to die. She was desperate to hear God's voice and not let the noise of her troubles keep her from hearing the voice of hope, God's voice. "Hey…hey…," the old woman tried to wake Sundaymah, only to watch her eyes peek and then drift back into slumber.

Sundaymah slept another three days.

For countless months, recuperation was slow, steady and excruciating. With the old woman's help, Sundaymah got stronger every day, week after week. Lousue Kai did the nurturing and God did the mending. Then one day, Sundaymah's heart found a resting place and she was willing to talk about her past. Ma Lousue had waited patiently to hear it.

What makes a man go so mad to be able to do such wickedness?

---

1    *Liberia's Independence Day, July 26th. Usually referred to as 26th.*

Maybe, some might say, it is because history gives him the chance. Liberian rebels, calling themselves soldiers or freedom fighters, had no regard for human life. For years rebel forces rolled throughout Montserrado and the rest of Liberia, terrorizing civilians—raping women and murdering men, women and children. Civilians were slaughtered even in the churches, a place of hope for the sorrow that invaded the lives of Liberian citizens. While the atrocity went on in Monrovia, there was little or no word about extended family members living in other parts of the country. The rebels roamed up and down Liberia and laid it to waste.

The first group of rebels invaded Sundaymah's neighborhood with false promises, presenting themselves as freedom fighters. This group did not rape or kill, but they stole everything in sight and moved on.

Several months into the war, life began sliding from bad to worse and a second group of rebels invaded their neighborhood. This group tortured and killed people who seemed worthless to them and all who resisted them. They watched in horror as one solider detached Sundaymah's father's arms and then slit through his throat because he'd refused to rape his own daughter on the rebel leader's order. Sundaymah had returned to find her mother and three sisters tortured and killed as well. She had been spared from the terror only because she had gone to look for food for the family. That week they slept with the stench of their loved ones in their nostrils, too afraid to be seen burying their dead.

She joined other civilians and they journeyed on foot from one neighborhood to another in search of safety, passing horrible scenes all around them. During this time Sundaymah came across a newborn baby in an abandoned neighborhood, lying in the middle of human bones, skulls and half-buried rotting bodies. During the entire year their kitchen was so bare one could not find a rat. Just providing for the basic needs of your own self was almost all anyone could do. Months of hunger had turned them into walking skeletons.

The times grew harder and the violence got worse. Boy-soldiers smoked marijuana and took other drugs, drank liquor, gang-raped old women and disemboweled pregnant women alive. Unborn babies were snatched from mothers' wombs to satisfy the rebels' bet on the baby's sex. Some rebels even ate human parts, becoming cannibals. But civilians adapted to life on the run; they got used to death in the streets, the neighborhood and how not to pay attention to sounds of shooting. People learned new ways to survive the rebels' attacks. Everyone bartered with everyone else and they traveled in groups.

After months of walking, searching for a place to stay, Sundaymah and fellow survivors reached an area near the Sinkor neighborhood. Most of the houses in the area had been damaged from weeks of rebels' aerial assault. This small group, Sundaymah, the baby she'd found and eight others, found the least damaged house and decided to stay a while. They were not worried about fatigue and hunger, but safety. They had not lived there for long. Early one afternoon, on the third day, they heard gunfire at a distance, a far distance, but they quickly dashed into the house and then to the ceiling, sitting silently, hiding in the ceiling crawl space of the house. The hiding space was so small, even a mouse would feel cramped.

The soldiers waited until the sun slipped behind darkening clouds when they entered the neighborhood. It was dark and quiet, not even a dog's bark could be heard. As they waited, hoping the soldiers would find nothing and leave, the child started crying, covering all other sounds.

"If that baby keeps crying, the rebels will find us and kill us all," one man complained in a whisper.

"What should I do?" Sundaymah asked, annoyed by the man's insensate nature. "There's no food…she is hungry."

"Then, I will kill you and the baby," the man sneered. "I'm not going to die because of that baby you found. She's not yours…you should have left her there."

All the women gave the man a disapproving stare although they knew he was telling the truth; the rebel would shoot if they knew people were hiding in the ceiling. Outnumbered, the man hissed and turned his head.

"Use your finger as a pacifier," one woman suggested.

Sundaymah did, but her finger did not quiet the child. The baby's blubber continued.

"Cover her mouth, for God's sake…they will kill us all," another woman suggested.

Sundaymah covered the baby's mouth, but removed her hand, thinking she might suffocate the child. The baby continued with her whimpering.

"They are in the ceiling," they heard a man shout. "I told you I saw people here. They are spies. Come, lets get those rats that are in the ceiling!"

There was a loud splintering sound below, and then gunfire. *Paw! Paw! Paw!* Everyone took off running, fleeing for their lives. Whirling around, the baby in her arms, Sundaymah pushed her way to the opening of the ceiling, praying the bullets would miss them both. She noticed an opening in the roof where a missile had landed days earlier and moved fast toward it. She felt the ceiling start to give way and pushed toward the roof. Crying through a burst of adrenaline and fear, Sundaymah climbed out and jumped. She hung in the air for a long time, still holding on to the baby. Sundaymah hit the ground and felt her knees buckled before rolling to a stop in the bushes.

The baby was quiet after they landed. Sundaymah checked the child; they were both covered in mud and blood. Her legs were screaming 'pain', but it did not matter; she had gotten them to safety, so she thought. It was only when a shadow appeared before her that she realized it was a man looming over her with his gun drawn. The man pulled the lifeless child from Sundaymah's grasp and flung it to the ground. At that moment, Sundaymah had no trouble processing what she was seeing. With chilling clarity, she knew what had happened; the baby had caught a bullet to save her, so the blood covering her was the baby's.

Sundaymah felt the man's hard punch, catching her on the cheekbone, knocking her to the ground. At the same time, soldiers jumped on the other six people before they had time to run away. They found out later that two other women had been killed, and the man who had threatened Sundaymah moments before.

The rebel leader, Creature, a name Sundaymah had given her rapist, looked more like a Rottweiler than a man. His large nostril was broader than round and he had dark brown colored eyes. Creature was not just unattractive, he was hideous. The man looked at her with rape intent and Sundaymah would rather take a bullet in the head than the Creature's touch. She gazed up at him pleadingly, but he grabbed her by the wrist, his hand trembling.

"You are coming with me," Creature shouted. Then, he told the others to take whoever they saw fit and ordered a small-boy[2] soldier to follow him. His orders were followed instantly.

Sundaymah kicked and fought while the Creature carried her off. When they got to his place, he ripped her lappa down to the hem and stripped himself from the waist. On his order, the young soldier watched while the Creature raped the woman. Sundaymah screamed from the bottom of her soul, but to no avail. When the attack was over, Creature withdrew himself, and got up. Sweat beads dripped from his face and body, looking at his victim, he had no shame for his desires. Sundaymah's eyes were clouded with tears.

"It's your turn," Creature ordered the young soldier.

Sundaymah guessed his age to be twelve or younger; for sure he was inexperienced, she could tell. The boy was overeager and climaxed before penetrating. He wasn't embarrassed until the Creature began teasing. To cover his embarrassment, the young rapist slapped Sundaymah hard across the face. Then with time, he learned to settle down; gaining more patience and during that time, he learned to be cruel. He spit on her, kicked her and stroked her breasts hard with his fist, as if they were punching bags. Fighting back was useless because Sundaymah had become weary and faint from exhaustion. Seeing she had passed out, the young rapist began to pet her rumpled hair like someone petting his dog. He was high on drugs. She opened her eyes only to remember his face even among thousands.

Her rapists killed her that night, but Sundaymah just didn't know how to die. She would have to wait until old age because everybody dies in the end. The next morning, tormenting pain helped her face embarrassment. She couldn't wait to wash the touch of their filth off her. Even after bathing with five buckets of water, their reek body odor still hung over her. Sundaymah swiped at her eyes, her fingers slick with salty tears, as she told the story. But the details of her troubles kept coming. She continued recounting her nightmare.

For eight months, they were the only people that occupied her world. She cooked, cleaned, and laundered for them. It was her prison. They repeatedly raped her, first the Creature, then the young rapist, in that order. Then, before falling asleep at night, they tied her to the bed so she did not escape.

---

2    Child soldier; military use of children under age 18 (some as young as 8 yrs. old) actively involved in armed conflict.

"One day, I stopped judging the men and judged God instead," Sundaymah choked. "I wanted to provoke God enough that He either send the Messiah back to earth right away or kill me. Then I asked myself, Is it okay to force God's hands?"

Rather than give an answer, Ma Lousue smiled and waited for more.

"Ma Lousue," Sundaymah said, her voice now whispery and hard to catch, "Was I being foolish?" Then gazing at Lousue Kai's face, she asked, "Was I too foolish to provoke God?"

The heartbreak in Sundaymah's voice was hard to miss. Lousue Kai's eyes were moist when Sundaymah finished, her heart broke over the wrecked condition of Sundaymah's world. She composed herself and whispered a prayer in her heart that God would help her know what to do and to say. Her compassion would offer whatever was necessary to heal the woman's hurt. She had found her for a reason and it was her belief; for everyone that seems lost, God sends someone to show them the way.

"No, child, you were not foolish," Ma Lousue said. "You were not foolish at all…just desperate. When troubles dominate your mind, you almost forget your faith. We must never forget in darkness what we know to be true in the light. It is difficult sometimes. At times our fears loom so big, we long for proof that God is actually there. When you are left with nothing…nothing but God, then you realize that God is enough. That's what usually happens."

Comfort came for Sundaymah in that hour, knowing she was no longer alone. Whether she liked it or not, life was moving forward. Her body became more of a living soul than a person she'd lost. She finally lifted all her fears into the wind to let it carry them away from her. After a long wait, she tucked away the rape in her mind and little by little reorganized her disrupted life.

****

Liberian women work hard, but have always been exploited by most men—rich and poor alike; during peacetime and wartime. Having a skill always increases a woman's earning power, thus giving her a chance for a better life. She must understand that survival is the only thing worth working on if a woman is determined to carry on with life.

Skilled in making fufu[3], Sundaymah earned a living selling fufu in the market while sharing Ma Lousue's home. She made fufu in pouring rain or under unbreathable dry heat, occupying herself solely with her fufu making business.

This strenuous task involves sorting cassava and selecting fresh, mature roots without rot. Then, removing all the skin and washing the roots in clean water to remove pieces of peel, sand, and anything else uneatable. The roots are soaked in water for 48-72 hours at room temperature and later, mashed into a paste. (a small amount of water is added to help dissolve it) The solution is then poured through a strainer to separate any stringy materials, which controls the size of particles in the fufu mash. The fufu mash is left alone until it is concentrated, and then emptied. This fermented paste is filled into sacks and placed in a jerk press to extract water. (large rocks are placed over the sacks to help it drain faster) Finally, the pressed starchy cassava mash is molded into soft golf-ball size paste and sold at the market as fufu.

Nick Anderson arrived in Liberia in the middle of the dry season, March. During the dry season, which is from December to May, the humidity rises so high, even walking a few yards makes a person feel as if he needs a shower. But in the unbeatable dry season heat, he saw women manage fires in sooty oil drums overlaid with wire screens as they spread fish on the screens to dry—they were making dried-fish to sell. Through the smoke and scorching heat, the women moved among the drums, flipping fish while they dry and blacken. Nick was touched by this and the many other ways he saw how people made the best of what very little they had. One evening while he strolled along the roadside of the city, he came across some women frying homemade pies in hot grease on fired coal-pots[4]. One woman persuaded Nick to buy her *meat pie*. The pies had no meat-filling, which Nick discovered after buying one. When he asked the woman, she explained it is canned mackerel she had sautéed in gravy and used for filling.

"You said this was meat pie, but it is not meat," Nick said, only teasing. "Why call it meat pie?"

"Good friend[5]," the woman said with a smile, "that's what we call it here."

---

3     *Steeping peeled cassava roots in water to ferment*
4     *A cooking device (similar to a grill)—raised iron bowl, some with a central grid—using charcoal.*
5     *An informal form of friendly address for a stranger*

"Oh…I see," Nick said, still smiling.

Whether it was drying bonny[6] fish, frying meat pies, or making fufu; such is the way of life for a lot of Liberian women trying to earn a living.

****

Nick had tried so hard to stick with only Americanized culinary— for health reasons—but he was craving authentic Liberian food more than ever. He'd eaten at the Cassava Patch, a West African restaurant in Norcross, Georgia and at different East African restaurants, so he was familiar with fufu and pepper soup. The silly thing is, he actually thought of preparing it himself. Nick did not know the labor behind the dish. Nick Anderson wanted to do something Nick Anderson had never dared, cook the food himself. However, authentic palate-pleasing fufu and pepper soup not only require culinary skills, it also requires the correct balance of the right ingredients.

Africa's markets are distinguished and run mostly by persuasive women traders who sell anything and everything that you will need. It was half past ten on Saturday morning when Nick reached the market. Like any other African market, Waterside Market on Mechlin Street evoked the sights, sounds and smells of the aromas of Liberian cookery. It was large, crowded and friendly as buyers, sellers and the smell of spices pumped life into it. Alongside in narrow alleyways, any and everything was at the market; skinned goats hanging on hooks, bushmeat[7], fresh fish and other seafood, dried fish, live chickens and ducks in small bamboo cages, various tropical fruits, colorful vegetables, edible roots, palm oil, potato greens, cassava leaves, Fanti prints and tie-dyed lappas, slippers and used clothing called *donkafleh* [8].

Market women never took a course in economics, but can determine selling prices; calculating their cost—fees for transporting their goods and cost of goods. Masters at buying and selling, they eke out a profit. For example, a market woman buys onions by the pound but sell them by size and not by weight. They understand that women

---

6       *Fish that is about six inches long and weigh about one or two ounces. They are too small when fresh and filled with small splinter bones. For the most part, the fish are dried for preservation.*

7       *Wild animals hunted for food; game and nongame animals*

8       *Imported worn clothes; most new clothes are far outside the affordability of the average Liberian.*

who prepare the family's daily meal buy an onion or two, according to the need.

Nick's soul seemed recharged by the market energy and humor as he strolled through holding a nylon shopping bag balled up in his hand. Sundaymah Boye saw Nick before he saw her. He was walking toward her stall, but the displayed blackened smoke-dried monkey meat on the table in the next stall held his attention. He bumped into a table before realizing he'd already reached the table where the fufu was. Nick looked at the woman sitting behind the table, she was smiling at him.

"Hello," Nick said, embarrassed. "I'm looking to buy some fufu."

"I got some right here," the seller said, furrowing her brow. How he could be looking for fufu when it was right before his eyes, she thought. She detected his accent and concluded the reason. "I'll give you good price, good friend."

"Okay," Nick said, "How much?"

"Five Liberian dollars for this much," she pointed at two piles. Each pile consisted of six molded white cassava mash, about the size of golf balls.

Nick did not know the currency exchange rate. "How about…I give you five US dollars and you don't have to give me back any change, would that be enough?"

"That's plenty…the rest is your dash[9] to me," she chuckled.

Nick had no idea what the woman meant. "Dash," he asked, doubtfully.

"Dash," Sundaymah repeated. She did not know how to explain it. It was usually the other way around. Market women always added a little more to the customer's order for encouragement.

"Okay, that's my dash to you," Nick agreed anyway.

While she put his order together, Sundaymah opened herself to the friendly stranger, "What's your name?"

"Nick…Nick Anderson."

Correctly connecting his twang, she asked, "Are you American?"

"Yes, ma'am…I am."

"I mean…are you Liberian but has come home or are you American," she probed further. She'd come across several *returnees*, a name given to Liberians that had waited for the war to end and had returned

---

9    tip

home.

Nick said, "American," and added, "I have no family here either."

"Who cooks for you?" Sundaymah said, skeptically. "This fufu you're buying, who is going to cook it for you?"

"I intend to cook it myself."

"Do you know how to cook fufu?"

"Well, I was going to ask you to show me how to cook it," Nick said, now more embarrassed. "It shouldn't be that hard, is it?"

Sundaymah laughed. No amount of instructions, no matter how many details were given, would Nick have been able to cook the fufu correctly. "If you bring it to my house, I will cook it for you," she offered.

Nick took her up on the offer and told her he would eat most things, except for monkey meat, which came as a surprise to Sundaymah, since it was sold in the market. He didn't mind some blackened smoke-dried fish, bonnie, for instance, which he didn't know by name.

"I know…no nyama-nyama[10] stuff for you," Sundaymah told him.

"Nyama…nyama?"

"Things you wouldn't eat," Sundaymah said. "I own some chickens, so I'll use only fresh chicken in your soup. The chicken is five dollars… US of course…I will use all of it."

Nick smiled, obviously at ease.

"I live across the bridge, in Logan Town. I'm here until five o'clock. Come back this afternoon around five-thirty so I can show you where I live."

"All right," Nick said. "Should I pay for the chicken now?"

"No," Sundaymah said, "You can pay me after I've cooked your food."

Nick returned in his rented Toyota Corolla at five-fifteen and waited to take Sundaymah home. She directed him to cross over the Mesurado Bridge, which connects central Monrovia to Brushrod Island, then onto United Nations Drive, the main road. When they passed the intersection to Somalia Drive, Sundaymah told Nick the road lead to the Monrovia-Kakata highway, if he ever wanted to go to

---

10    *Liberian conversational term for 'plenty' different items, anything and everything edible to expand and/or season a dish; pepper pods, kitili, bitter ball, okra, shrimp, tiny fish, etc*

Kakata. When they bypassed Jamaica Road, she told him Boatswain Jr. High School was off that road. They finally reached Logantown Road and then the house. His offer to take Sundaymah home had rewarded him with a grand tour of "across the bridge". He'd never been to that part of Monrovia.

Sundaymah's home was a modest, but decent, four-room house built with bricks, set on a strong foundation. It had corrugated metal sheet roofing and concrete slab flooring. The veranda was attached at the entrance of the house, partly enclosed. The bathroom was a separate small shack in the back, divided into two sections; one was used as washroom to take bucket-baths and the other an outhouse, an enclosed room with a two-hole wooden seat over a pit, serving as the toilet. The only running water was a community well shared with other families one mile up the road. Sundaymah paid teenage boys to fetch water, which they toted, several gallons on top of their heads until the drum in the kitchen is filled. They had no electricity, but owned a few kerosene lamps, candles and flashlights.

While the African kitchen is traditionally outside or in a separate building, as most food dishes entail slow cooking and extended prep time—meat and fish is marinated for long hours, spices and grains pound in the mortar, large amount of leaves chopped, fresh fish scaled and gutted, to name a few—the kitchen in this case occupied one of the four rooms, the smallest. It was clean and neat with defined space with several areas that had places for several various sized pots and pans, a storage place for large rice bags, condiments, a table space for prepping and dishwashing and a cooking area where two large coal-pot stoves sat.

Sundaymah introduced Nick to Ma Lousue and the two instantly bonded. Nick sensed the old woman had maturity and patience on her side because she took her time to learn his name and said it with proper pronunciation. She had an infectious smile and her eyes were filled with warmth, as if she was playing a role that had been imposed on her.

After the quick tour of the house and yard, Ma Lousue led Nick to the veranda and offered him the hammock. She sat on a rattan chair. Without hesitation she asked why he had moved to war-torn Liberia, still with wretched roads, paltry markets and ruined houses. Even several years after the war, Monrovia still had no good plumbing and those with electricity seldom turned their lights on. Only those who could afford ownership of a diesel-run generator had electricity. Nick had chosen Liberia because during the early eighties his father served as a Peace Corps Volunteer teacher in Grand Bassa County, he told her and the other reason; it seemed cool to be in a country where an elected president was a woman. His eyes twinkled when he said the last reason. The thing about fate is, which the old woman already knew, life is unpredictable and at times dreadful.

Was it possible to look healthy and then be told you have six months to live? Death is that last journey everyone takes alone. Nick Anderson had been given his death sentence in his doctor's office days after he'd had a seizure at work and was rushed to the emergency room where he had a second seizure. With cancer in his family history—his father had died of colon cancer, his mother, from breast cancer and his only sibling, a younger brother, from leukemia—his doctor suspected the worst. After a few tests, they found a mass in his lung and several lesions on his brain. Nick had stage IV melanoma cancer that had spread to his lungs and brain. The melanoma had traveled beyond the regional lymph nodes and metastasized to his brain and lungs. There is no stage V. It seemed crazy, he looked healthy and his doctor was telling him he had less than a year to live, with treatment—radiation, chemo, etc.

The fact was, no medicine could help Nick, his doctor told him, but medicine is not everything. The doctor advised Nick to do the things he'd always wanted to do. He should focus on increasing the quality of his life based on the five-year survival rate. Actually he had at least six months, or a year if he was lucky.

How was he to bring a sense of purpose back into his life again? Like the way to manage his life's savings he will no longer use or the way to make a living in his fifties when it no longer mattered. His desire to meet someone he'd marry wouldn't be fair to her. To be honest with himself, that desire ended the day his doctor diagnosed his illness. Nick wasn't sure he'd see Christmas, let alone become a father, watch his children grow, marry and have children of their own. Melanoma cancer had cut the natural order of things and cure was so far away. *I'm dying,* he'd whispered to himself, *How can I even think about those things?*

Thirty-two-years-old and armed with the knowledge he had less than a year to live, Nick Anderson wasn't going to sit around waiting to die. Conventional wisdom urged him to wage war on the disease. Instead, Nick decided to make each day an opportunity to experience God in his life. He would search for God while he waited to die. Nick arranged with his lawyer, who recommended an American doctor he could see while in Liberia and here he was.

When Nick finished his story, he caught the old woman staring at him and sensed the sadness she held in her heart for him.

"I'm not looking for a miracle," Nick said, "just a chance to do something good for someone else before I die."

It was their first meeting, but Lousue Kai put her arms around Nick's neck and hugged him like a mother hen gathers her chicks under her wings. "All humans are not born bold," she sobbed in his ear. "But you, Nick…you are very brave."

A mother's tears are so powerful that they soothe everything in its paths. A sweet mother hugs her child to reassure him. The child feels less frightened, covered with a peace no storm can disturb. Nick felt Lousue Kai's teardrops on his neck. Whether she knew it or not, her marvelous talent to love injected in him more courage than a free-roaring lion had.

The next day when Nick returned to the house, he met Sundaymah straining to lift a 50-lb bag of rice onto the shelf, an ambitious feat for an independent woman. She'd raised it only a few inches off the floor, but her eyes were determined and her face carried the effort.

"Let me help you," Nick offered.

Together they heaved the bag up, each holding on to an end, onto the shelf. After that, Sundaymah checked the coals in the coal-pot stove. She leaned over the stove, blowing on the coals.

"I'm about to cook your fufu," Sundaymah informed him, "You can watch if you like. You want to learn to cook it, right?"

She was only teasing, but Nick decided to watch anyway.

Sundaymah dissolved the molded fufu balls in cold water and strained it to get rid of any solid cassava particles. She poured the mixture into the cooking pot and set it aside. This was done to settle it, she informed Nick. When the fufu sediment had settled at the bottom of the pot after twenty minutes, she showed it to Nick. Sundaymah then poured the liquid out, leaving only the fufu sediment in the pot. She placed the pot on the fired coal-pot stove, stirring the fufu constantly with a wooden spoon until it thickened. When the fufu had changed from a white starchy consistence to firm clear-color dough, the texture became thick and heavy. As it cooked, it became more difficult to stir.

Sundaymah explained the fufu was cooked and removed it from the pot and into a large pan for cooling. As soon as the fufu reached a tolerable temperature, she used her hand and shaped it into a sizable portion of mass by repeating folding over, pressing and squeezing the dough. "A sprinkle of water is needed to free the dough from the pan," she explained and turned the dough over, smooth side up, in a serving bowl.

The fufu looked like a masterpiece of art, Nick thought. He found the fascinating variety of a different culinary tradition to be over-whelming and laborious, thus he quickly reconsidered cooking his own fufu.

"Next time, you will cook it while I watch," Sundaymah teased.

Nick smiled.

Liberian culture, being so rich and diverse, collectively elevates food to a peculiar status. Liberian dishes are never bland. The meals are undeniably appealing to the senses; the taste tantalizing, the aroma exciting. These dishes are rich in spices, mostly peppery and with unique flavors difficult to describe in words. Traditionally, such culinary knowledge is acquired through years of apprenticeship in your mother's kitchen. Sundaymah had indeed demonstrated her culinary skill as far as Nick could tell.

Besides Nick's dinner, Sundaymah also prepared the family evening meal; rice and potato greens. He did not understand why she'd cooked so much food when only she and Ma Lousue lived there. Little did he know, in Liberia, there is always extra food available in case a caller comes by; be it a relative, neighbor or stranger. He watched Sundaymah dished out some rice into a large bowl, and then poured over the heap of rice a large amount of greens cooked in palm oil. She called for a young boy, about eight years old, and he came running. She explained she'd always cook extra food to give the neighbors' children something to eat.

The little boy took the pan full of rice outside to the backyard and five younger children, boys and girls, followed him until they were under a tree. They sat around the big enamel pan, buttocks low to the earth, knees cupped in armpits, bodies rocking on splayed feet in a flow of eagerness and joy. Dipping their hands in the same bowl like siblings, which they were not, their little elbows swung out as tiny fingers curled the rice into balls greasy with palm oil. Nick could see satisfaction on Sundaymah's face as they watched her little neighbors' chins become slick with red palm oil.

Sundaymah finished cooking the pepper soup, hardly using any pepper. She arranged Nick's food on a large tray and placed it on a small table on the veranda. Also on the tray were three small saucers with bennie[11] seed, boiled bitterballs[12] and boiled mashed okras. These were condiments for the pepper soup, especially the bennie seed, which has a nutty flavor and great aroma.

"These *nyama-nyama* here…you can eat," Sundaymah said, pointing at the condiments. "They will add more flavor to the soup."

She showed Nick how to embellish the pepper soup with the condiments, by taking a small portion of each and mixing it in the soup. He quickly learned how to eat the dish; making an indentation on the edge of the dough, tearing off a bite-sized piece with the spoon and scooping up some soup with it. Nick stuffed his mouth and began chewing.

"That's not how you eat fufu," Sundaymah corrected. "You have to swallow it whole."

"Why…you don't chew food in Liberia?"

Sundaymah chuckled and said, "We chew rice, not fufu."

The fufu had a slightly sour taste to it, because of the process of fermentation, but Nick's taste buds were exclusively directed to the tasty pepper soup. Little did he know the mystic of pepper soup; it can be as equally tasty when prepared with very minimum ingredients or if prepared with every conceivable element that could be added to a dish. The supreme companion for the fufu was magical. Nick had never had any soup to taste that good. All other dishes seemed insipid. From then on Sundaymah cooked his meals.

Nick did not bother with the treatment of a clinical trial[13] which his doctor had proposed, often recommended that stage IV melanoma patients participate in, that may help them with their symptoms;

---

11    *Sesame seed roasted and pounded into paste.*
12    *African eggplants; grow to about the size of golf balls and resemble a miniature, globe shaped pumpkin.*
13    *A research study meant to help improve current treatments or obtain information on treatments for patients with cancer.*

headache, fever, fatigue, nausea, vomiting and pain. Before coming to Liberia, Nick had searched for and hired Dr. Mellody Douglas, an American doctor at JFK Hospital, for palliative therapy, treatment given to relieve the symptoms and reduce the suffering caused by cancer; as needed to improve the quality of his very limited life. At first she'd started him on Dacarbazine injections to slow the growing cancer cells, but the side effects—loss of appetite followed by headaches—became unbearable. Dr. Douglas switched Nick to 960 mg of Zelboraf tables—four 240 mg tablets twice a day and the side effects were more tolerable.

By April, after one month in Liberia, Nick had learned many ways of Liberia; the handshake for instance. A Liberian-handshake ends by snapping the middle finger of one's hand against the middle finger of the other participant. A snap is made that sounds like a strong popping-click noise, when the fingers part. Nick greeted everyone with the handshake, practicing it over and again, until he had perfected it. "The Liberian handshake," he announced each time he did it right. During pastimes, Ma Lousue taught Nick some of the traditions, customs, philosophy and wisdom of all the Liberian tribes in their rich folklore, consisting of parables and proverbs.

****

Sundaymah didn't have to hide behind any mask because Ma Lousue had told her she was not at fault for the crime committed against her. She could not have controlled the actions of those heartless men or other people. She should never feel ashamed. But shame is like a wall that separates a rape victim from other people. It is almost impossible to let someone get close to you if you think you don't deserve to be cared for. It is a painful emotion from the consciousness of something dishonoring, especially when you feel your reputation has been injured. You reject yourself, believing you are unwanted and unloved. Most women are strong emotionally and the determined ones are much stronger.

Sundaymah tried, not allowing shame to be shackles binding her to her past. She and Ma Lousue were family by chance and now she had a real friend, Nick Anderson, someone who laughed and made jokes about the way Liberians do things. Nick had pointed out that Liberians always answered a question with another question, giving an example. Someone would ask, "Are you coming to my party?" And the other person's answer would be, "You want me to come to your party?" When Sundaymah heard it, she agreed with heartfelt laughter. It had been so long since she'd experienced something so easy and natural. They were connected in many ways. There was sadness within him he could not disguise and the thing about it was, it matched hers.

An incredible bond grew between Sundaymah Boye and Nick Anderson. Her friendliness toward Nick and his toward her could only be described in the words of Oscar Wilde, *"Love is all very well in its way, but friendship is much higher."*

****

Sundaymah did not have education in her head, but she had plenty common sense. She could recite her ABCs, but didn't know why they mattered. For one thing, she didn't know the alphabet had sounds. Nick could not imagine anyone going through life without being able to read. Being a skilled reader, he had a gift that could change Sundaymah's life if he taught her how to read and she was willing to learn. Nick suggested, if Sundaymah wouldn't mind, her going to night school. He'd pay her tuition. Boatswain Jr. High School was across the bridge and not far from the house. They even offered adult literacy classes at night. Sundaymah flatly refused and drifted away every time Nick brought it up. He wasn't going to settle for her negative response though and decided to teach her himself. One day Nick showed up ready.

"I told you, I don't want to learn to read," Sundaymah stressed, headstrong about her decision. "You brought the ABC book anyway."

Nick ignored the reprimand. "I also have flash cards…they will make learning fun," he said and sat in the chair across from the hammock where Sundaymah was sitting. Her gesture and words passed by him. "I want to help you," Nick insisted.

Nick understood she'd been consumed by horrible frustration. Like him, everyone had been taken from her and life had not always been kind. He was running out of time and his pain medicine would only hold him for so long. He wasn't dealing with ego, he was lucky. She gave him a look Nick interpreted to say she wanted him out of her way. But he wasn't going to wait until Sundaymah was ready or the next day.

"You can do this," Nick encouraged, ignoring her hesitant movement. "Okay," he pleaded.

"Okay," Sundaymah agreed, with a childish pout.

Nick noticed there was a sadness she still carried.

"Good," he said, smiling.

Sundaymah quickly shook the sadness off her face, something she'd gotten good at.

"Don't you miss America?" She asked, changing the subject, still trying to throw him off track.

"Sundaymah, I don't have much time," Nick blew out a frustrated breath. "It's important that we start and finish the reading lessons."

Sundaymah started to say something but lapsed into silence. Nick sighed.

"What's so important about me learning to read," she said out of frustration. She made eye contact with Nick, but did not maintain it.

"Because chance favors the prepared mind," Nick said. "Always be prepared for an opportunity." He paused for a breath and said, "Do not be afraid, Sundaymah, you will learn to read, I promise."

Sundaymah considered Nick's point. He was good at steering *easier said than done* conversations toward easier ground. There was no way she could talk him out of teaching her to read. She'd tried. Sundaymah surrendered and agreed to a schedule. The lessons were to start the following evening, no matter how he felt health wise.

****

With most of the work behind, Sundaymah enjoyed sitting on the front porch, talking with Ma Lousue. They did not own a radio so their evening chitchat was their only indulgence.

"When time passes, it carries a part of you with it," Sundaymah said, crossing her arms. She seemed to carry a lot on her mind this night.

Ma Lousue correctly considered it to be about Nick Anderson. "Which part of you has been carried away," she said.

"The appetite for things…Nick…all these strange things he is bringing to my ears. I don't want a father…or a husband," Sundaymah said, with stubbornness in her voice. "I accept our friendship, but there are too many expectations."

Sundaymah was stubbornly independent and the old woman

already knew this.

"So stop fighting for what you've lost," Ma Lousue said. "Start fighting for what you have left."

"What do I have left?" Sundaymah asked, keeping her gaze forward and her head down.

"Hope," Ma Lousue answered. "Leave hate…forget the disappointments…grief…tears. Live again, Sundaymah…put your life in God's hand and trust Him. Maybe this is the new life God has set for you to find."

"Life with a dying man," Sundaymah protested.

"Maybe," Ma Lousue said. "The heart has its own sickness, you know."

Sundaymah uncrossed her arms and lifted her head. She'd started listening to the old woman's words.

"You must free it, Sundaymah," Ma Lousue continued. "Free your heart and forget all the wrong done to you so you can leave those inner chains that keep you half-free and half-bound. God wants you to turn from the dull despair and set your heart free. Live your life and share the happiness Nick wants for you. This will make things new."

"I don't know how," Sundaymah admitted. "Nick wants all those things that are impossible."

"Well, when you do the impossible over and over…it becomes the possible."

Sundaymah shook her head with disagreement. "Nick wants to teach me to drive, can you believe it," she said. "But I told him no. What will learning to drive do for me? I can barely afford a taxi, where will I get the money from to buy a car?"

"He also wants to teach you to read and write…you said no… why?"

"I don't know," Sundaymah admitted. "What will that do for me? The time for me to learn to read is finished. I know the numbers. I know how to count so no one can easily cheat me with money."

"It's not about the reading and the driving," Ma Lousue pointed, "It is hope."

"Hope for me?" Sundaymah sneered. "Shame has no hold on some people, but it has some hold on me. Does he not know a defiled woman remains as such for life? It's a one way ticket, you know. You think I resent destiny, it's not so. In my case, how can I fight against both humiliation and death? I can beat neither of them."

"If being a victim is a one way ticket, then don't turn back," Ma Lousue said. "You keep going to your past. Everybody has a past, Sundaymah, you cannot change it…you can only learn from it. God does not walk away even when it seems so. You, of all people, know. By the way, the right man is on your side. Nick has hope for you when you don't have any for yourself."

Sundaymah kept her peace, considering the lecture.

****

Nick was determined to teach Sundaymah to read in six weeks, he'd do so by combining children's books with reading games and activities. The reading lessons settled into something of a routine, every night after Sundaymah finished her housework. Ma Lousue did not mind losing her evening company on the porch. And each time before Nick started, he constantly reminded her of all the reasons literacy was useful and important. By learning to read, she would be given a gift of confidence, self-respect, better economic opportunity and a better life. She was already a market-savvy woman, a natural entrepreneur. He was helping her turn that into solid assets, adding another stitch of hope in her life to help her move forward. Nick accepted her occasional silences and varying moods, and he was patient and diligent; coming back with new ways to make learning enjoyable.

Learning to read at forty-one is difficult. Nick began at the letter A and emphasized letters and sounds, connecting the letters to speech. It wasn't an easy task, but progress was made and that was important. Sundaymah struggled with reading and there was nothing Nick wanted more than to work hard at helping her succeed.

After five weeks he'd heard her read at the second grade level, but only by herself. Either she was shy or rebellious; but Sundaymah refused to read in front of him or Ma Lousue. He knew what her answer would be if he'd simply asked her to read for him. He had a better idea, a perfect plan.

Summoning his courage to test Sundaymah's reading, Nick laced his fingers together when he sat. "Will you go to the store for me?" Nick asked, staring at Sundaymah.

"Yes," Sundaymah said, without giving much thought.

Nick handed her a list and Sundaymah was caught by surprise.

She thought all he wanted was one or two things. If he'd expected her to read it, she already knew she wasn't going to. Sundaymah looked at the list, and for a split second the demon of failure confronted her, teased her; even challenged her. She couldn't say no. Bringing back everything on the list was all she had to do, a voice told her and she would have passed his test. She was not easily fooled.

"The supermarket or Kollie Shop," Sundaymah asked.

"Go to Kollie Shop," Nick said, handing her some money. "Take a taxi and have the driver wait for you. Hire him for three hours…that should be enough to cover the trip."

Kollie Shop was a few miles from the house. The old retired schoolteacher had used money his children sent him from America to open his small shop which offered items people most likely ran out of—sugar, baby milk, salt—things people need not take public transport to go to the supermarket or general stores. He also carried local specialty items the general stores didn't stock, which kept his small business afloat.

Mr. Kollie was checking the shelves when Sundaymah walked in. She greeted him and handed the list over. Mr. Kollie unfolded the piece of paper and read the first line. Above the list Nick had written that he expected the woman to give him, Mr. Kollie, the list, but he, Nick, wanted the bearer of the list to read it herself. The sentence directed the merchant not to give Sundaymah anything unless she'd requested it by reading it herself. Mr. Kollie handed Sundaymah back the list and smiled. He said nothing. Sundaymah has no education in her head, but she has plenty sense. She suspected Nick had done exactly what she was thinking. Retrieving the list, she held Mr. Kollie's stare for a moment before forcing herself to turn away.

"I will get the things as you read the list," Mr. Kollie said, pulling out a small box and placing it on the counter.

Sundaymah starred at the list. Sensing her discomfort, Mr. Kollie began rummaging around behind the counter. He then began straightening can goods on the shelves giving her more time to study the list.

A few minutes went by. Mr. Kollie cleared his throat and said, "Just let me know when you're ready…take your time."

Sundaymah studied the list for a while longer, read the first item on the list, "*coffee*", using syllables, as Nick had taught her—part of the word is pronounced with a single, uninterrupted sounding of the voice. A written word can often be divided, he'd told her; they hold together to make sense. She remembered.

Slowly, but surely, Sundaymah read from the list; (three packs) chewing gum, (four cans) sardine, (ten) maggi cubes, (six bottles) coca-cola, (five cans) mackerel, (two cans) corned beef, (four whole) smoke fish, (one bag) peppermint candy, (one pack) sugar, (two cans) blue band margarine, (one pack) needle, (one can) Ovaltine, (one can) Nido milk, (one) comb, (three packs) Marie biscuits, (three cans) evaporated milk, and (two whole) stock fish.

Mr. Kollie put the things in the box, one by one, following Sundaymah's reading. She read the last item on the list and peeked in the box.

"That's all," Sundaymah said, shrugging her shoulders, feeling a little sheepish. She had done it!

"Good…you did well," Mr. Kollie said proudly.

Sundaymah counted out her bills and handed the money to him. Mr. Kollie took the money, tapped the keys and the register drawer opened with a ring.

"It's heavy, I will have the boy take the box to the taxi for you," he said and gave her the change.

"Thank you," Sundaymah murmured; her voice apologetic. She left the counter when a young man, about sixteen, took the box off the counter.

Sundaymah reached the house and took the things to the kitchen. Rather than unpack the groceries, she went to the porch to find Nick instead. He was waiting with a big smile covering his face.

"You made me shame," Sundaymah greeted Nick with an accusation.

"I did not make you shame," Nick said, still smiling. "You were supposed to read the list without anyone's help."

"I didn't ask for his help," Sundaymah rebutted.

"You didn't have to," Nick answered, now giggling. He didn't mind being busted.

"You called, chicken soup, maggi cube[14]?" She chided, getting back at him. "Was that to trick me?"

Nick chuckled. He had not tricked her; it was another *Liberian*

---

14    *Individually wrapped chicken bouillon cubes for base in soups and sauces; comes in beef and vegetable flavors also.*

thing he'd discovered. Liberians referred to the flavor of the item rather than by its brand name. Maggi cubes came in beef flavor also, but it was not referred to as beef soup.

Sundaymah shook her head, thinking she had gotten Nick back. She was not angry with him, she couldn't have been. There was no malice found in his doing. *Okay, it's official*, she thought, *I can read*. She was happy, but didn't show it.

****

June started with light rain. Nick was lying in bed at the hotel thinking about Sundaymah, about himself, and about a lot of things. For a moment, he thought about his first car and remembered the feeling when he got it; a gently used Honda Civic his father bought him when he was promoted to the eleventh grade. He got it washed every weekend and kept it clean. The Honda always looked nice. He'd cruised around with his friends while they listened to rap and RB music with a lot of bass that thumped through the speakers. Nick knew how to have fun without being wild and crazy.

It will be different for Sundaymah, he thought. She'd have learned a new skill and passed a driving test, a major milestone in her life. Plus, she'd have more freedom than she had in the past. He thought about buying a more fuel efficient car for both short and long distances; but a car suitable to generate income, which involved highway driving. Sundaymah could use the car to transport goods for the market women instead of working so hard, sitting in a stall all day, to earn a few bucks. It was also important that Sundaymah felt comfortable in it which was not too much a concern. He would find a way to boost her confidence. The next morning Nick turned in his rental and bought a truck, a 2009 Toyota Land Cruiser 70.

On Sunday afternoon Sundaymah was sweeping the porch when Nick drove into the yard. She squinted, to her surprise, spotting Nick behind the wheel. He'd always taken a taxi when he did not have the rented car. She leaned the broom handle against the banister and ran out to the yard.

Nick climbed out of the truck. "Look what Saint Nick bought you before Christmas," he said, pointing at the silver Toyota Land Cruiser 70. There was a big yellow bow tied to the steering wheel.

Sundaymah looked at the bow. "Why is a big ribbon bow tied to the car wheel?" She pointed at the steering wheel, her face serious.

"Do you like it?"

Sundaymah blinked. "Do I like it?"

"There you go again, answering a question with a question...you Liberians," Nick chuckled. "I'm going to teach you how to drive it."

There was a pause.

Sundaymah glared at Nick, he watched her face as shock gave way to confusion. She opened her mouth but said nothing. For a long moment all they could do was stare at each other without moving. Neither of them said anything. When Nick spoke, his voice was soft.

"I know it's big, but when you get used to it, it wouldn't seem so big," Nick said, reading her mind correctly.

Sundaymah eyes held his, wavering before they finally dropped. She sighed. "Let me call Ma Lousue," she said, her voice subdued.

Ma Lousue stepped out onto the porch before Sundaymah open her mouth to call. Even from a distance, Nick noticed an expression of contentment on the old woman's face. It did not seem his doing had surprised her at all. She smiled and waved, volunteering no more.

Nick escorted Sundaymah to the passenger side and helped her in, and then he slipped behind the steering wheel on the driver side.

"You need to put on your seat belt," Nick said, looking at her, as if to say, *Are you ready*?

Sundaymah gave him her bravest smile.

"Okay, let's go," Nick said.

There was tenderness in the way he taught her, a depth of patience even she had not quite expected. They drove every road within five miles of the house three to four times. Like most beginners, Sundaymah struggled to keep the truck moving straight. She had trouble with over-steering; she veered into gutters on the side as pedestrians rushed out of the way. Balancing the truck on a hill was impossible to do, as she tried to find the correct balance of accelerator and clutch. Nick found it hilarious. She couldn't help giggling as well.

As weeks of driving lessons wore on, Sundaymah felt a little relaxed, but still was not confident she could actually take full control of the truck. Sitting behind the wheel of any car was dangerous, especially for pedestrians as she did not trust herself. That was the word she used, trust. It would kill her if she hit another human being.

Nick handed Sundaymah the keys to the Land Cruiser 70. "That comes with practice," he said, his tone encouraging. "The more you drive it, the more normal it feels."

It was not a consideration; Nick had actually bought her the truck. Sundaymah still had trouble believing it, even as she held the proof in her hand. He also bought her a radio so they could listen to the news and a cell phone to keep in touch while he was away. Since the day of their meeting, Nick's visits to the house started with the neighborhood children running to meet him, each tugging at his pants while he handed out treats; chocolates, candies and biscuits—which are cookies. Then he always presented Ma Lousue and Sundaymah something, body lotion, perfumed soap or an apple, an imported fruit they had never eaten until they met Nick. He gave and gave and gave again; spending himself and not counting the cost.

Despite the misfortune they'd both gone through, or still going through, this was nothing but an ordinary time for Nick and an extraordinary time for Sundaymah. It was hard to find meaningless-ness in anything he'd done. Sundaymah even felt a sudden unexpected surge of hope. Then, maybe, just maybe, it would not be possible to experience similar days in the future. She almost forgot Nick was dying.

Sundaymah tried to enjoy the good times while the demons were sleeping. But fear is the enemy of the soul and it is fear that kept reminding her bad things are not far behind when good things happen. All the good things happening could actually stop the next day, and tomorrow she'd fail. Sundaymah wished she could erase her memories of the bad things forever and never have that failing feeling again.

\*\*\*\*

Ma Lousue watched Nick leave to go home on a late rainy night in July and suggested he spend the night. The next morning, the old woman told him to go to the hotel and pack his things because he was moving in with them. That night she'd watched a young man looking old, old and lonely. He'd lost his entire family, but she did not believe he was destined to be alone. That's why he and Sundaymah had met, she thought. Coincidence had not pushed him here. Their lives had started a world apart and fate had taken the distance from between them. Nick felt secure with them and knew they cared about him as well, and that is why he accepted Ma Lousue's proposal.

Time, unfortunately wasn't making it easy to stay on course, considering it was not an ordinary beginning. The path Nick had taken was straight as ever, but it was filled with aches and pain. The cancer was overtaking his life hurriedly. He wasn't strong and certainly not healthy. His days were spent like a car running on fumes, desperate to make it one more kilometer before running out of gas completely. He continued taking increased doses of medication to help offset the heightened pain he was feeling. The pain intensified, and at times even raising his arm made him grimace. He tried to move about normally, as long as his heart kept beating.

There was no rain on the third night in August, even though it was the rainy season. The evening was cool and crisp, the sky absolutely clear without a hint of clouds. Through squinted eyes Nick looked at his watch. He realized it was time for their evening walk, it wasn't raining and he wanted to make it, feeling sick or not.

"It's a beautiful night for strolling, isn't it?" Nick said standing, then shuffling across the porch to the entrance.

Sundaymah looked at him and smiled. "Yes, it is. But, are you sure you can handle a walk tonight?"

With thoughtful look in his eyes, Nick took a deep breath. "Well, yes, I think I can," he said, smiling slightly, as if he was holding a secret close to his heart.

Sundaymah looked at him, wondering whether to believe him. She knew he was faking it because Nick moved at the pace of an old man now. In recent days he'd barely touched his food and he'd lost more weight, even in the last week.

They followed their regular routine, slowly walking toward the halfway mark on Logantown Road, which was about one mile. Nick seemed stronger, and they walked a little farther in silence. Just ahead, a dog trotted across the road, stopped and lifted one hind leg and relieved himself against some bushes. Nick cracked a joke that the dogs don't care where they mark their turf, they just do. Then they walked passed the same small group of market women who were always sitting by the roadside roasting cassavas and plantains on fire coal-pot stoves for waiting customers. They saw Nick and Sundaymah and exchanged greetings. One woman sold parched groundpeas[15] and *sweet mother*, which Sundaymah explained to be small plastic bags of frozen kool-

---

15     peanuts

aid. Nick laughed at the fact there was no comparable connection that a frozen flavored ice had with a mother. He liked the name though. If the women ever wondered about Sundaymah and Nick, Nick would not know. They said nothing directly to Sundaymah or Nick, only exchanged smiles and greetings. Those were normal scenes from everyday life which made him feel better. Nick tried so hard to lead as normal a life as possible for as long as he could.

****

The days continued to pass and the progression of Nick's disease continued, speeding up as September gave way to October. The disease weakened his body, preying on his muscles, making even simple things more difficult. Sundaymah noticed the pounds wasting away. Nick's face was growing thinner and the boniness of his fingers became more obvious. He was never hungry and when forced to eat, he took small bites and chewed for a long time. Soon walking became difficult for Nick, unless it was only for a short distance. Of course, he walked only if he could put up with the pain, which sometimes he couldn't.

Week by week, there were noticeable changes in Nick. The left side of his body started to get weaker and he started taking longer and longer naps. Usually he would fall asleep within minutes of a conversation, and Sundaymah would stare at him, afraid to leave in case he needed her.

"Nick," the sound of Sundaymah's voice jarred him awake. "Should I call Dr. Douglas? Maybe she can give you something to help you."

"No," he said, half awake, forcing a smile.

Sundaymah often studied Nick, wondering how her life would have been had they not meet at the market. When he spoke about his family and how each had died of cancer, there was neither bitterness nor self-pity. There had been some sorrow, of course, and some loneliness in his expression as he spoke of his mother, comparing her to Ma Lousue. Beyond that, she could not easily read his feelings. And sometimes, in the moments before sleep, she wondered if Nick had ever judged God the way she had.

The next day, Nick nursed his bottle of Fanta as they sat on the porch where Sundaymah had set his dinner. He'd barely touched the pepper soup, his favorite meal.

"Are you having another headache?" Sundaymah asked, deeply

concerned.

Nick didn't answer right away.

"Nick...."

"I'll be okay, Sundaymah," Nick whispered.

Stifling her tears, Sundaymah could not help but think about her life. Time had started to run backward, she thought. Then the thought came into her head like music. She got up, went inside, found the book Nick had given her, and then return on the porch with it and the dictionary. After sitting down again, she looked at the book. It was old, the cover was torn, and the pages were stained with age. It was *Murder in the Cassava Patch* by Bai T. Moore. Sundaymah let the book open randomly and read the words to Nick: *I would pay the full dowry required for a virgin, ten pounds sterling, or forty dollars. The procedure involved the following: twenty-five cents, to find out from the family if there was any other suitor besides me, if no other suitor, twenty-five cents to shut Tene's ears to any further requests from suitors; two dollars to tie the rope on her hand, or engage her, fifty cents to cut the rope or confirm the engagement.*

Sundaymah finished, struggling with few words, mostly those she'd never heard; like *sterling* and *procedure*. Nick wasn't surprised. He'd watched her workday and night, slaving so hard to make fufu, selling at the market, cooking their dinner, and then practicing her reading lessons; barely with any time to catch her breath. People do that for one reason, to succeed. He wished she'd practice driving like she did reading.

"Read it from the beginning," he murmured, forcing a smile. "This time you don't need the dictionary, I will help you with the big words."

Sundaymah smiled to herself. After five months, even she could not believe how she had developed with her literacy skills. Though she had rebelled against his idea, she was glad Nick had insisted. Like so many Liberians that never had the chance, or some like her who did and wouldn't take the opportunity, they lived their life and never looked for change. They just grow old with whatever life throws at them.

Ma Lousue joined Sundaymah and Nick and the three spent part of the evening on the porch listening to Sundaymah read the story about Tene and Gortokai. Ma Lousue found it amusing that the man in the story had a name that sounded like hers, Kai.

Another week went by and Nick grew steadily worse. Dr. Douglas was there for Nick, visiting him every other day now. Sundaymah stopped selling at the market, sitting quietly beside Nick's bed during his waking hours. It saddened her heart seeing him bedridden, looking smaller, almost like a little boy again.

****

On the first night of December, long after everyone went to bed, Sundaymah could not sleep. Thru the window, the sky was filled with moonlit clouds. She tossed back the covers, got out of bed and walked to Nick's room. She sat beside his bed and watched him for a long time. Nick had something beautiful showing on his face, it was kindness. That's what she saw, kindness; not sickness, not pain, not death. Part of her wanted to cry right then, instead, she took his hand.

"Sundaymah," Nick whispered; his breathing shallow and weak.

"Yes, Nick…I'm right here."

He tried squeezing her hand, his grip weak, looking at her. "You are going to be all right," he said, his voice slightly above whispers. "Call the doctor tomorrow morning and tell her…just tell her to come."

Sundaymah turned away, but Nick could see the tears in her eyes. Part of him wanted to cry too.

"You want to know something?" He asked, his eyes pleading with her for understanding.

Sundaymah didn't answer. A pit formed in her stomach, her mouth felt dry and she felt her heart pounding. It is over, Sundaymah thought. She knew this was the evening Nick would leave her. This was the hardest part of their friendship, saying good-bye and he'd be gone for good. Nick had forced the best out of her and it had made her better. People are their best when true friends get behind them. She felt better. And, besides, life is not measured by the number of breaths we take, but by the moments just before it is taken away.

"You helped me with so many things, Sundaymah…you did. I'm happy…you've made me happy," he whispered.

A lump rose in her throat, Sundaymah became speechless. She turned her head for a moment, only for a moment, and when she turned back, Nick's breath had left him, just like that. Sundaymah did not cry, she did not scream.

"Ma Lousue…Ma Lousue," she called in a soft whispery voice.

Ma Lousue was already standing in the doorway waiting, giving Sundaymah time while thinking about what to say. Then, she walked to Nick's bed.

"Sundaymah," Ma Lousue said. "God's will is done in the help we give each other. This is God's way...you are not going back to your past...you are not." Then she prayed in her mind, *Oh God, you better not make a liar out of me.*

Sundaymah dialed Dr. Douglas's number on the cell phone, it was seven-thirty in the morning. Dr. Douglas arrived an hour later and arranged to have Nick's body taken to Turay's funeral home, where other arrangements would be made to fly his body back to America for burial.

One week earlier Nick had handed Sundaymah two large manila envelopes. One had been addressed to Dr. Melody Douglas, another had no name on it and it remained sealed. He asked her to promise him she wasn't going to open it until after his passing. Sundaymah handed Dr. Douglas both envelopes when she got to the house. The doctor opened the one addressed to her, and then she opened the other envelope with no name. The contents were addressed to Sundaymah and Mr. Robert J. Douglas III, Nick's lawyer. Dr. Douglas advised Sun-daymah to keep the envelope until RJ, Dr. Douglas's brother, arrived in a few days.

The following week, the lawyer was escorted to the house and intro-duced to Sundaymah and Lousue Kai. While Sundaymah explained how she and Nick had met and how their friendship had helped her more than it helped him, the heartbreak in her voice was hard to miss.

Sundaymah felt oddly consoled sitting in front of Nick's lawyer. The man was friendly, telling the details of the envelope contents over and over for Sundaymah to understand. It was Nick's will. He had left some money to pay for Sundaymah to finish high school, and even go on to college. Some of the money was to help take care of Ma Lousue, have electricity and plumbing added to the house when the time came. The lawyer was to pay out the funds at the proper time. It was up to Sundaymah, whatever she wanted.

****

On a crisp Sunday morning, eight days after they had witnessed Nick's casket loaded onto the Delta Airlines plane and taken back to his world, Sundaymah sat in the clear morning light on the porch with Ma Lousue. They were sitting in silence, enjoying the light breeze and the warmth of the sun. Sundaymah seemed stuck with the pain of losing Nick. Once more there wasn't any more. She felt the sorrow rising but forced it back down.

Ma Lousue noticed that tears had welled up in Sundaymah's eyes. It was expected for Sundaymah to grieve over Nick's passing, but not an insane grief like what she did for her family and the baby she'd found. Nick had made her promise she wouldn't grieve, but rather celebrate his chance God had given him.

"Sundaymah," Ma Lousue said, "What are you thinking?"

Sundaymah looked up, the old woman's lips had formed a delicate, but a distant, smile.

"Man is nothing but a handful of earth," Ma Lousue whispered. "Remember what Nick said…don't look back at what is lost."

"Nick," Sundaymah said softly, and her lips smiled a second later. "If I keep doing what Nick wants me to do, there will always be more ahead."

Ma Lousue liked hearing that.

Then, Sundaymah suggested, "Let's go to Kakata."

"Kakata," Ma Lousue said, staring with a long blank gaze. "Who will take us?"

"Me," Sundaymah answered. "I will drive us there," she opened her hand and showed the keys.

Ma Lousue looked at the Toyota Land Cruiser 70 parked in the yard and back at Sundaymah. "With that car?" She pointed. She wanted to remind Sundaymah how adamant she had been about the truck being too big. Sundaymah always described the truck with that word, *big*. She chose not to. Instead, she said with a chuckle, "Sundaymah, promise not to kill me today," and got up.

Sundaymah waited to see whether the old woman would go to the truck or back into the house.

"Well…let's go," Ma Lousue said and started ahead.

"I intend to do the impossible over and over until it become the possible," Sundaymah said as they walked to the truck.

"Don't kill me while you're doing it," Ma Lousue teased.

Ma Lousue climbed into the front passenger seat and Sundaymah got into the driver seat. Both women closed the door.

"Seat belt," Sundaymah reminded Ma Lousue, the way Nick always used to.

Sundaymah looked down at the floorboard, "clutch, brake, gas," she counted the three pedals in her head. Then she shifted her attention to the gearshift on her right and studied the simple diagram on the top. The diagram looked like a three-legged H, like Nick had described for easy retention. First, third and fifth gears were at the top of the legs; second, fourth and reverse gears were at the bottom. The crossbar of the H is neutral; she remembered.

"Are you sure, Sundaymah," Ma Lousue said.

Sundaymah nodded and checked the parking brake to make sure it was engaged. Then, she pressed down the clutch pedal and moved the gearshift into the crossbar section of the H. She turned the key and started the engine. Both women's rapid heartbeats yielded to the roar of the engine. Ma Lousue looked at Sundaymah and gave an approving, but doubtful, smile.

Keeping the clutch pedal down, Sundaymah moved the gearshift to the top-left position, dropping the gear into first. She applied the foot brake and released the parking brake. Ma Lousue looked ahead and waited for the truck to move.

Ready to start moving, Sundaymah released the foot brake. She released the clutch pedal slowly and at the same time, slowly pressing down the gas pedal. She pressed down the gas pedal and continued to release the clutch. The truck started to move forward.

"You are taking us to Kakata," Ma Lousue cheered, half-scared and half-happy.

Sundaymah smiled. She accelerated until the truck reached about 3,000 RPM, then she took her foot off the gas pedal, pressed down on the clutch and pulled the gearshift directly down, through neutral, to second gear. She released the clutch pedal gently, simultaneously pressing down the gas pedal. Sundaymah repeated the shifting process until she was on the main road driving at the correct speed.

*I am actually driving*, she thought and looked down at the gauges on the dashboard, squeezing the leather-covered steering wheel, as if admiring the power at her disposal—the beast of steel the truck was built of. The instant her eyes left the road, she felt the car zigzagged.

"Sundaymah," Ma Lousue gasped, stretching her arms forward to hold the handle on the dashboard in front of her.

"We are okay, Ma Lousue…we are good to go," Sundaymah assured her. "I just took my eyes off the road for a second…I won't do it again."

"*Sundaymah, drive with your eyes on the road,*" she heard Nick's voice in her head. "*Stay focused on the road ahead to assure you of a car traveling a straight line.*"

She complied with Nick's instructions with telling result— the silver Toyota Land Cruiser 70 drove straight ahead, proudly displaying SWEET MOTHER stenciled in bold black letters on the sides.

*From the writer's pen*

People seldom know what they want or what truly matters until they get what they ask for. Then half of the time they don't know what to do with it; not knowing when *sufficient* is *enough*. Before you know it, pride builds a nest in your soul and suddenly, the wear and tear of life isn't much of a challenge. But building your life according to your own instincts is never good enough, often resulting in a bad outcome. You break apart and find yourself in need of starting over again. This time, with a keen sense of how important God's directions are, you follow the blueprint for a good life. You do it by humbling yourself, giving to the needy and responding with love to those who have wronged you. And then sometimes it takes a miracle to fix things, that is, if you believe.

One might agree (or not agree) a miracle is an event or something which man is not normally capable of making happen, which is therefore thought to be done by God. A miracle happens so a worthless life can be sent into reverse—this is my opinion, of course. Whether you believe in miracles or not, we certainly do not deserve it, or rather, can earn it. Nevertheless, thank God for second chances.

# Believe

A narrow dirt highway passes through Pleebo, connecting Montserrado County from Monrovia[1] to Harper, Maryland County. There are no lights that change from green to red in Pleebo, but the earth there is rich and matted with grass. The soil holds the mist and rain that seeds into it. It remains beautiful, almost holy, as it came from the Creator. It is tended and guarded by nature to keep God's man fed and nurtured, especially people with skills but no jobs nor any means of lifting themselves out of poverty. Hardship of poor people is incredible.

The palm[2] oil tree is native to large parts of Liberia. It is a tree of life, a symbol of joy and for most events, a festive decor. Its fruits feed man, and its branches clothe and shelter, providing the three basic human needs. A palm branch has over fifty blade-like leaves. One leaf can produce a strong string by peeling away the solid green substance that makes up most of the leaf, thus leaving about eight or nine threadlike fibers more than two feet long. These threadlike fibers are placed on the thigh and rolled with the palm of your hand, twisting them into a piece of thread. These strings are woven into fishing nets.

Buildings in Monrovia are like those in other modern cities, but huts, (framework similar to that of any structured bungalow) are usually built for occupancy in the villages. The hut walls are built by

---

1    *Liberia's Capital*
2    *A full-grown palm oil tree can reach a height of about 60 feet; a single, erect, ringed trunk and bearing at the top, a crown of large dark green pattern leaves resembling the structure of a feather. Each may be 15 feet long, with leaflets 2 ft or 3 ft long.*

arranging sticks made from the central stem of the palm branch, in a cross-bracing grillwork to hold the mud plaster in place. The whole palm branch, folded over and stitched closely together in bands, makes thatching[3] for the roof of the hut. Like shingles, one band lays on top of another to make double thickness of the palm branches.

The climate provides the hottest and tropical conditions under which these palm trees flourish. Many areas around Pleebo have a long tradition of managing palm oil trees, but cutting palm nuts is not an easy job. Traditionally, this is a challenging professional occupation. Before the palm tree is climbed, the climber must check to make sure the tree is not sick and is strong enough to be a magnet for the climber. Great strength and skill, as well as knowledge and intelligence, is needed. The man must know how to climb a palm tree with or without a rope[4]; barefoot and barehanded. Like rock climbers, he pulls and pushes on his legs in opposition against the tree.

Palm nuts[5] (palm oil tree fruits) are borne in spiky bunches called heads, which are small and many when the tree begins to bear, from the fourth to the eighth year, and larger but less numerous as the tree becomes older. Each tree, from about 10 to 30 feet in height, is calculated to bear at least seven funnels of palm nuts. Full bearing under good conditions, the yield is between 8 to 10 bunches. A bunch can sometimes weigh 25 lbs., or even more, and contain about 750 useful oil nuts.

Palm oil production is an intricate task. It is hard and demanding work to extract oil from the palm fruits. This method consists of the following steps: treatment of harvested bunches, separation of fruit from the stalk, boiling of the fruit; fruit pounding, oil extraction from the pulp mixture, kernel separation of pulp mixture, oil clarification, and kernel drying. Once the palm oil is extracted, the black hard kernels left are used to make kernel oil. A career in palm oil production is not only tough, but dangerous too.

---

3      *The palm thatch provides a cool and dry interior when it is sunny. During the hot weather, the palm thatch dries and curls up, permitting the air to pass freely. During the rain, the wet palm thatch quickly expands and closely flattens to keep the rain out.*
4      *rope made of twisted palm fronds*
5      *The palm nut fruit is no larger than a grape, but has a central nut (kernel, which is used in making palm kernel oil), enclosed by the soft juicy pulp from which red oil is made.*

\*\*\*\*

"It is as if my husband's heart died within him and he became a stone," Nyeneplu complained to Helena over the cell phone. "I admire Youwah Saytue because of his ambitions and I also pity Youwah Saytue because of his pride. He refuses to listen. Because of his pride, Youwah no longer knows where he stops and God starts. He has refuses to become humble and does not see that all things are in God's hand. As long as Youwah refuses, God will show him. Now, it has taken something like this to happen to him, so he might bow to God on his knees. With his own tongue, he will make the confession; 'God is king in my heart, not me.'"

"It will happen, Nyeneplu, just keep praying," Helena encouraged.

This was after telling her sister about Youwah's accident.

\*\*\*\*

Pride is such a liar. Youwah Saytue did a bad thing by boasting in his arrogance and God caught him. That's what people were saying about Youwah after his accident. 'He is a good man, but he likes juju[6] business too much'.

"But no one can figure out the way of God," Nyeneplu corrected them.

Nyeneplu also thought God had caught her husband. She prayed every day for God to hush her husband's spirit into peace and chase pride from his heart.

When we desire something, the heart longs for it. When we get it, we fear it; not knowing what to do with it. Nyeneplu prayed for a husband who would love and care for her. She got that man, Youwah Saytue, who loved his wife as much as he loved himself. What Nyeneplu had a hard time dealing with was her husband's arrogance. The man had more ambition than anyone she knew in all of Maryland County.

If anyone in Pleebo thinks he has reasons for confidence in himself, even if he has reasons for confidence in his own ambitions, Youwah Saytue has more. He was born the first son of a paramount chief in Pleebo/Sodoken District, Klebo Chiefdom, and a Liberian Grebo. As to zeal, Youwah is the most successful oil producer in the town and as to place in the community, an upright citizen in Maryland County. No one can accuse Youwah Saytue of owing a debt not paid.

---

6    *The art to invoke supernatural power*

Saytue started his palm oil business with just his cutlass[7]. The African forest gives many different products, including the palm oil tree, and this is what Saytue studied when the idea to make red oil to sell came to his head. Besides the red oil, palm kernel oil is also produced and is profitable. Youwah was smart in this understanding to invest his energy and time in the palm oil tree.

What's more, climbing the tree is a mission seemed impossible to most. This was Youwah's greatest asset, mastering the skill. He possessed a magnificent coordination of posture and movement, redistributing his body weight between limbs. This created a force under his feet during the climb, a basic climbing strategy among expert climbers. Then, armed with the cutlass, Youwah Saytue is able to use both the right hand and the left hand when chopping wood, clearing bush, or cutting any palm nuts bunch. This ability made the perception of a successful oil production feasible.

"I want to help you invest wisely in your future," Youwah said to his best friend, Wakla Wesee, as he began his talk about the palm oil business. "Investing in your time will be profitable. Our hard work will give us the best return for our future."

Long after that day, Youwah and Wakla achieved a friendship of equal understanding, in both business and personal affairs. In business, their hard work granted them the means to take care of their families. This was a way to escape poverty and the shame in begging. Youwah and Wakla made every effort to supplement their labor. They even employed five other men; Wakla's three grown sons and Youwah's two nephews. There was brotherly care in the men's labor that kept them effective and fruitful in producing the oil. Each man was more diligent in doing his share of work. For this practice the quantity grew, so did the profit.

The men start oil production first by walking a small trail for about two hours to reach the place where the wild palm oil trees are plentiful. They gather palm nuts from these trees. Youwah climbs the tree without a rope (most climbers use a rope) and then trims the bottom branches before cutting the heads while the others are responsible for gathering the palm nuts as they fall. The men collect these nuts in large baskets made of stripped palm branches while the whole

---

7     *A short, thick, curving knife with a single cutting edge used for cutting down sugar cane, dense underbrush, etc*

bunch of palm heads is placed in kinjas[8]. The nuts are then taken to the campsite, strategically close to the house, where the process of oil making begins.

At the processing camp, fresh nuts are cut from their bunch and left spread out on the ground for a couple of days—to ripen further. The nuts are then boiled in two barrels. Youwah had purchased these used oil barrels with his own money, proving his belief in the business. After twenty-four hours of cooking, to soften the fruit and reduce water respectively, the boiled nuts are transferred into another barrel for pounding—this barrel is fitted into a pit for mortar[9]. The men used long poles as pestles[10] to separate the pulp and trash from the nuts, working together to crush the nuts completely to get the oil out. They continued to pound the nuts until juices began to flow out of it. Then, the massive mushy mess of crushed nuts is transferred to a washtub[11]. Cleanliness makes the oil good, so Youwah had encouraged his team to use a washtub instead of a pit in the bare earth, a method other oil producers use.

Next, the mashed nuts are soaked in hot water to separate the oil from the fiber. The water-oil mixture is then put into cooking barrels to remove the water completely. Importantly, Youwah makes sure the precise amount of fire is put under the cooking barrel to keep the mixture hot, but not too hot, otherwise the oil will not be good quality. During this process, the water settles at the bottom and the oil separates and floats at the top. All the small bits of palm nutshells and fiber are filtered out, thus producing high quality oil.

Once the oil is extracted, the women, led by Nyeneplu, use the black hard kernels left to make kernel oil. This darkish, nutty smelling oil is used for hair, skin and also to make soap. Children have their share of the palm nuts too, by taking these kernels to a set of stones set up for the purpose of kernel cracking. The kernel is placed on a stone and hit with a smaller stone and voila, the nut inside is obtained for snacking.

---

8      *Double-waved baskets—two feet in diameter—made by plaiting palm leaves together; kinjah comes in various forms and serves multiple purposes. As a container, it is used to carry produce or to hang food for drying.*
9      *A vessel or receptacle used with a pestle to soften or grind substances*
10     *A long, slender piece of rounded wood (pole) used to pound or grind substances in a mortar.*
11     *A round 35-gal galvanized zinc wash tub.*

Youwah easily met his potential. He and his crew extracted close to five tons of oil each year, exclusive of kernel oil. He made higher profits by selling the majority of his oil during the off season, which is between September and December, when oil supply on the market is low. During these months, the price of red oil increases by more than 100 percent.

Youwah also saw the ripple effect of their hard work in the local markets, supplying oil to market women. Hardship of common people is challenging, so this granted them the ability to feed their families and also educate their children selling his oil. For this, Youwah was looked upon as someone with authority, having much influence on the women as he did on the men.

There were other palm oil producers, but none as successful as Youwah Saytue. In three years time Youwah had earned more money than most, taking care of his family—aunts, old uncles, cousins and nephews. The family ate twice a day, instead of once a day like many other families. Youwah also took care of extended family members besides his wife and son, Gyebo Saytue. His business made it possible to send Gyebo to live with Helena, his sister-in-law, in Monrovia to attend school. The boy had reached the ninth grade, the furthest anyone in Youwah's family had reached. Youwah believed that as his business continued to grow, it would eventually direct the boy's steps to the university.

Another big plan of Youwah's was to improve things for himself and the family. He'd build a modern house with a modern bathroom in Montserrado County and move the family there. This was not merely a dream. Youwah's house in Monrovia already had a foundation and the walls had started to go up. Building this concrete house was supervised by Helena, with the money Youwah sent her each month.

Wakla enjoyed the same success, but had no plans to leave Maryland County. He had already finished his concrete house in Pleebo, though a small one. Wakla did not mind that his concrete house did not have a modern bathroom either, as long as it had a zinc roof that also covered his porch.

"I don't have to move to Monrovia to enjoy my success," Wakla said to Youwah one day. "Every morning I take pleasure in watching my wife sugar my tea. Because of this business, I drink tea every day like the kwi[12] people."

Youwah laughed at his friend's inclination.

\*\*\*\*

People always remember the worst days of their life because they become part of them forever. Climbing a palm tree has a dark side since accidents are part of climbing. Accidents happen—mistakes or mishaps—and it can be unforgiving. That day, it seemed Youwah did not take a stand for safety. The most important thing to remember during a climb is to travel cautiously, especially a twenty-foot African palm oil tree. Climbing it, your safety—or lack thereof—is totally in your hands.

Youwah is always awarded with something far deeper than access to the palm nuts when he reaches the top. Not only does he enjoy the sweeping views of the forest, but the satisfaction of a physical conquest as well. With every climb he is swept with an emotion he describes as, "Getting closer to fulfilling his dream and giving Nyeneplu the decent life she deserves."

The sensation of the task is also a worthy reverence to him. Before the start of every climb, Youwah would rub the stone that the local medicine[13] man, Geesayglocon, gave him to wear around his neck, asking the tree for permission to climb. He believes the climb goes a lot smoother that way.

"Be smart, be careful, and take the necessary precautions," Geesayglocon advised him, when he placed the stone around Youwah's neck. "Do not visit the dark side of this job. You must learn caution so that you live to climb another day."

Month after month, Youwah climbed effortlessly; every time with his regular ritual, until the day of the mishap. That day he rubbed and kissed his stone, as usual, recited the plea Geesayglocon taught him and began the climb. Half way to the top, something dreadful happened. It happened fast. Youwah felt his feet slip, then his hands. His cutlass fell first, escaping his armpit; and then, he followed. Images began to disconnect, all too fast for any warning.

The impact was violent, hitting his chin on the way down, then

---

12      Citified, as in having the sophisticated style or manner associated with an urban life style.
13      A person, like a witch doctor, who is supposed to have the power of curing disease, warding off evil, etc. through the use of supernatural power.

crushing his toes on the hard earth. Youwah landed hard on his backside, cracking a bone in his back. There were broken bones in both legs and his right foot, plus three of his toes. Blood gushed from Youwah's chin where he'd suffered a deep cut.

Wakla nearly fainted, thinking his friend had died. He managed to calm his nerves and put his wits to better use by quickly plugging the hole on Youwah's face to control the bleeding. Blood needs to clot in order to start the healing process and stop the bleeding. With this in mind, Wakla tore a piece of cloth from his t-shirt to use as gauze, and placed it directly on the wound, applying pressure. Blood quickly soaked through the dressing. Wakla tore off a second piece and applied it with pressure. He did this four times, leaving each layer in place. While Wakla attended Youwah's wound, the other men hurriedly braided palm leaves into a toting kinja. Using the kinja as a hammock, they carried Youwah on their shoulders to the main road to wait for a car.

The men did not feel as if they were doing *plortor*[14] work, as in toting hammock. Youwah was one of them and they were executing the best and fastest way to get him to the hospital. It was not a long wait when a private pickup approached the crew. They flagged the driver to a stop, loaded Youwah in the back and off they went to J.J. Dosssen Memorial Hospital in Harper.

After his release from the hospital, friends and relatives piled onto Youwah's porch daily to wish him luck in getting well again. His injuries had left him disabled, for the most part; Youwah was unable to do much for himself. He no longer walked on his own and his wife managed his daily personal care.

In the months that followed, Wakla kept Youwah buoyed about the business, visiting with him every week and giving reports on the sales as well as taking advice on maintaining it. Happy to see his friend, Youwah's toothy grins always seemed welcoming until the day their conversation drifted to the accident and God. Wakla's visit on this day seemed purposeful. He joined Youwah on the porch soon after exchanging pleasantries with Nyeneplu.

---

14    *Liberian slang for labor that is degrading, as in toting hammock. While there were no means of automobile travels in rural Liberia, men from the village were used to tote government officials, from village to village, in a hammock. Such labor is humiliating, especially when these citizens had not benefited from their taxes paid to the Liberian government—no roads built, among other things.*

The men sat alone.

"Youwah," Wakla started, "maybe you ought to draw nearer to God so He can lead you to a better road."

Meant to be a simple, friendly advice, Youwah furrowed his brow. He waited for his friend to go on.

"God wants to see good in your heart," Wakla continued.

"So, Wakla, you are telling me there's no good in my heart?" Youwah asserted right away.

"You once had good in your heart, Youwah, but not anymore… not since the accident," Wakla said, pruposefully keeping back details of his thinking.

Wakla was referring to his friend's adamant belief of Geesayglo-con's medicine. The old juju doctor was demanding from his friend more white chickens, more white sheep, more this and more that. Youwah, too, was more than willing to part with more of these things.

"You, too, believe that God has caught me?" Youwah asserted. It seemed a tone of contempt.

Wakla sighed and said nothing more.

"Wakla, mind your mouth," Youwah snarled. "You continue to forget who made you successful. Just remember from whom you get your money. I do not want to remind you, maybe I need to. From our childhood, isn't the medicine man the person that has made all the sacrifices so we can be competent and equipped with the courage to work hard?"

"I used to think that way, Youwah, but not anymore," Wakla answered.

There was a pause, enough time for Youwah to collect his thoughts.

"Why," Youwah asked, and then baited, "Is it my wife or your wife that has spoiled your mind?"

"Both," Wakla quickly answered. "Your wife taught my wife and my wife taught me."

Youwah chuckled. "You would rather listen to those women instead of listening to the person who has shown you the road to success," he said.

Wakla read his friend's remarks as bragging. "For true, Youwah, I traced your steps and they were strong to follow," he replied. "And, while we were making the oil, I humbly scrubbed the pots and pans and I did everything your voice ordered. Just because you've directed my feet to success, that does not make you the beginning of my world. Do not think that you hold my life in your hands."

Touched by this, Youwah replied, "Wakla, I do not own you, that's true. If it seemed that way, it was not intended to be. I am sorry."

Wakla nodded, accepting his friend's apology.

"I enjoy the blessings every day and I am grateful for all of it," Wakla said. "But, who gets the credit; Youwah, God or Geesayglocon?"

Youwah made no answer. A deep frown etched in his forehead as he stared at Wakla's face.

"You are a good man, Youwah," Wakla continued. "I see you greet everyone with an honest handshake. Your 'yes' is always 'yes' and your 'no' is always 'no'. You've always paid us on time and with fair wages. Success is sweet in all of our mouths, not just yours. Don't you think because of your pride, *what is* has become *what was*?"

"The success you claimed to enjoy today is because of the sacrifices Geesayglocon made on our behalf," Youwah pointed out. "Is it not so?"

There was a pause.

"Well," Youwah baited.

"Riches and honor come from God," Wakla declared. "That's what I know."

"God?" Youwah snarled.

"Yes," Wakla said, his voice assertive. "God reigns over all. Power is in God's hand and only God can make a person great. God gives the strength. When God gives you these things, maybe He is trying your heart."

"There is no reasoning with you, Wakla," Youwah accused right away. "All I hear from you people is God…God…God. You people can believe in whatever you choose to believe. I know it is Geesayglocon who has petitioned for my success all these years."

"So, Geesayglocon is your protector?"

There was a pause.

"You cannot say it," Wakla continued. "Youwah, you cannot say it with your own mouth."

"Geesayglocon is not my protector," Youwah said, defiantly. "The things he does for me is what protects me…not him."

"Then what happened to it that day?" Wakla said. Realizing he'd said something he had not wished to say, he continued, "Maybe your protector was sleeping that day…the day of the accident. When God is your protector, He never sleeps. That's why in Liberia we say, 'God don't sleep'.

Youwah's face was now a clenched knot. A long pause hung between the friends and silence followed. Wakla sensed a thought was forming in his friend's mind. Rightly so, Youwah was cranking up his anger. Then, it poured out.

"You've come here to mock me," Youwah accused. "It is true, Liberians are a jealous people. You get small success and they wish to see you fall. I was someone you used to listen to when I walked around on two legs...just like you. Now, your God has caught me and I am nothing to you."

Wakla gasped, being accused. His insides locked up tightly. "Youwah, it is not so," he pleaded. "It is not so...."

Youwah stared past Wakla, holding up his hand, signaling he was not finished speaking his mind.

"I want you to leave," Youwah emphasized, waving Wakla off. "Don't come back here, Wakla...do whatever you wish with the oil business, just go."

Youwah alleged other hurtful things, expressing mostly the disappointing and disloyal conduct of his friend. Wakla waited patiently until the man was done ranting. It was obvious they had reached the limits of each other's tolerance. Wakla was out of ideas and Youwah was trounced by his frustration. Wakla stared at his friend's face, allowing Youwah's words to sink into him. Then, ever so slightly, Youwah bowed his head. Youwah was finished, so it appeared. Without saying a word, Wakla walked out, perhaps wondering if there had been some mistakes. After all, his friend had dealt wondrously with him in the past.

After Youwah's brief meeting with Wakla, he gave his wife the silent treatment for a day or so. He'd blamed her for *spoiling* his friend's mind. "Why are you always harassing people about your God business?" Youwah accused. In response, Nyeneplu simply adopted an innocent look and flashed a smile. She also kept her promise to stay out of Youwah and Wakla's affair, after sensing the spark between the friends. But Nyeneplu's pampering began to charm Youwah once more and he was chatting with her again.

****

One evening, several days later, Youwah was unusually silent while

Nyeneplu got him ready for bed.

"My darling husband, would you like anything before I turn in for the night?" Nyeneplu asked, as she was leaving the room.

"Tomorrow, I want you to send for Geesayglocon," Youwah demanded. "Now look. I do not want to hear another word about your church business. What God will not do for me, I will do for myself."

When the woman's brain caught up with her husband's voice, she could not believe what she was hearing. Does Youwah really think a man can do what God will not do? Does he not know that God can actually stop the world from going on? It is no use explaining to a fool what he does not understand, she thought.

"Youwah, do not expect good to come here as long as you are cutting God off," Nyeneplu daringly warned her husband.

"I am not cutting God off," Youwah argued. "Every time Geesayglocon gives me his medicine, he says 'if God agrees.' That's not the same thing?"

"No."

"Why is that?" Youwah furrowed his brow. "God is nothing but a word."

Nyeneplu covered her ears with both hands. "God is just a word," she choked, repeating her husband's blasphemous remark. "Youwah, that Word is alive...that Word is powerful," she said and put down her hands.

There was a pause.

Youwah sensed intolerance in the woman's voice. He certainly did not want to get into another argument with her over God business. He knew well enough, Nyeneplu never backed down when it came to her religious belief.

"It's a small price I pay when I give Geesayglocon the white chicken and the small sheep to make the sacrifice for me," Youwah said, pleadingly. "His medicine will heal me, Nyeneplu. It's a small price to pay for my healing. Why can't you see it? Why are you still complaining?"

"It is not about the money you are spending," Nyeneplu replied. "I do not care about the money, Youwah. There is no power in the blood of those animals that Geesayglocon kills on your behalf. Those sacrifices are useless," she stressed. "Healing powers are only in the blood of Jesus."

"Then let Jesus come so Geesayglocon can kill him," Youwah

chuckled.

"You have the nerves to challenge a God who spoke the world into existence," Nyeneplu warned, not cracking a smile. "Do not take the privilege of life for granted, Youwah. God is almighty."

Youwah shrugged and waved her off.

Nyeneplu walked away, leaving Youwah alone about her God business. However, she wasn't done, that fight was far from being over. Nyeneplu spent the rest of the week fasting and praying.

On the day Nyeneplu ended her fast, she called Helena using her cell phone. In a tearful plead, Nyeneplu begged her sister to come to Pleebo, and if possible, to bring the man of God who had told all these things about Jesus. Helena responded with a promise to try and advised Nyeneplu that they both would pray about the request. The women prayed at the end of their lengthy conversation before saying good-bye.

Julius Peabody's rickety old Toyota pickup rattled out of Montserrado toward Maryland, starting on the Monrovia-Kakata highway. After hearing the bad news about Youwah's near fatal accident, Helena's pastor agreed to take her and her nephew to Pleebo. The old pickup sputtered and stalled during local driving so a few months had passed, three to be exact, before the trip became possible. Pastor Peabody patched up his old pickup and soon they were ready for the trip on a very bad road, rendering it difficult to travel, at mostly thirty miles an hour through a moonscape of potholes and mud. The trip takes about ten hours in the dry season and maybe sixteen hours at the beginning of the rainy season. On this trip, the old pickup took twenty-two hours to reach Maryland from Montserrado, passing a few towns and villages along the way.

****

Nyeneplu prepared her husband to receive his visitors—changing the beddings, taking out the dirty dishes, dressing him, and then placing chairs to accommodate the guests.

Helena led Pastor Peabody to her brother-in-law to introduced him. *Herein lies the challenge*, Helena wanted to say. Instead, she made the proper introduction, "Youwah, this is my pastor, Julius Peabody."

"Hello, Mr. Saytue," Pastor Peabody acknowledged his not-so-happy host. The man looked like he'd never smiled his entire life.

"Thank you for having me in your home," Pastor Peabody continued gleefully.

Youwah replied, "Reserve your gratitude until you've heard what I have to say."

Nyeneplu started to reprimand her husband because of his impoliteness, but Pastor Peabody held up his hand, stopping her. He did not need her help, the Holy Spirit was there to empower. Pastor Peabody believed that the reward for witnessing to Youwah was all worth the risks of rejections.

Pastor Peabody said, "Mr. Saytue, I understand your frustrations. I am here doing God's work, which is to hold my brother up when he has fallen. So, there is nothing you can say or do to humiliate me. I am here to serve you."

Youwah sighed. He furrowed his brow.

"Never give up hope, Mr. Saytue," Pastor Peabody continued. "If you do, all that is left to have is despair and bitterness."

A reasonable person faces the music, even if he really hates the tune. Youwah had no choice in this case.

"What makes you think I've given up hope," Youwah challenged.

Pastor Peabody caught Youwah's bluff. It is hardly possible to state with sufficient clairty the importance of the leadership role of a pastor. A role that is pivotal if his work is done with consultation, collaboration, and with sensitivity to the views and needs of others. His work is to help advance the mission of Christ. The spiritual lives of this family was now entrusted to him, a noble task requiring devotional energy and faith. Peabody prayed that with God's help and his human efforts, the reward would be the transformation of the man and the growth of God's kingdom.

Pastor Peabody saw that misery was clearly visible on the man's face. "And, there you had me worried," he said to Youwah, in a jovial tone.

Settling his ego a notch, Youwah dropped his shoulders. "My wife told you many things about me, maybe she left out my accomplisments," he said. "I am a man who is very proud of his accomplishments. I can boast of them because they're all around for people to see. I've always worked hard, more than any man I know. You see, Pastor Peabody, I am who I am...Youwah Saytue."

"I know," Pastor Peabody agreed. "And, God is who He is."

Nyeneplu thought it was best to intervene and clarify her husband's hardheadedness.

"Youwah has always feared what would happen if he sat still and stopped working," Nyeneplu explained. "He has worked all the time because of this ambition. I believe something bad has happened because he refuses to see God in his success. It is his pride, I presume. Youwah no longer knows where he stops and where God starts. I believe that God still wants to heal him while he rests, but Youwah would not listen."

"My success," Youwah snarled. "Is it God or my own ambition? Am I being punished by your God because I want independence?"

"Oh God...oh God," Nyeneplu petitioned, tapping her chest with her hand. "Forgive my husband, Lord, forgive him. He is foolish. Youwah is innocently foolish. I beg for your mercy."

"Youwah, it is foolish to ignore God," Helena jumped. "God is calling you, but you are not answering. God is trying to preserve your life!"

"Mr. Saytue is right," Pastor Peabody interrupted.

This drew an instant gaze from both women, a puzzling stare.

Pastor Peabody said to Youwah, "Maybe God has put this accident into the rhythm of your life for a reason. Maybe it is because of your success, then again, maybe not. Sometimes when someone begins to see himself as more important than he is, he needs rest to see clearly."

"Rest?" Youwah challenged. "You are calling my illness a rest?"

"Perhaps," Pastor Peabody alleged. "Thank God you did not die... you could have died. Mr. Saytue, each day that God allows us to see is a second chance."

"What a second chance," Youwah snarled. "So where is God during my trouble?"

"My husband does not have a hearing heart," Nyeneplu jumped in. "He is not willing to trust God with this suffering."

Pastor Peabody turned toward Youwah. Youwah shrugged.

"See," Nyeneplu pointed. "In this house, I alone live with a faith in God. They say Faith cleanses the heart, don't they, Pastor?"

"Yes," Pastor Peabody nodded.

"Then, I will be the one to find the good in our suffering," Nyeneplu continued.

"Where is the good?" Youwah snarled.

"The good is there, Youwah, but you are not willing to see it,"

Nyeneplu challenged. "As for me, I will rejoice in it."

"Your praising of God in our troubles has not turned our burden into a blessing, has it?" Youwah asked.

Nyeneplu smiled.

"Well," Youwah baited.

"You wait and see," Nyeneplu replied. "You will see the good, despite your hardheadedness or the circumstance surrounding us."

Youwah heaved a sigh and closed his eyes, under pretext of being tired. The truth was, he was dissatisfied with their preaching. Then he began yawning and stretching.

Watching Youwah, Helena saw her brother-in-law as someone who had been drained of much of his strength and energy through exertion or boredom, when rest or sleep was essential.

"Youwah is worn out, maybe we should let him rest," Helena suggested.

Nyeneplu detected her husband was faking this exhaustion. She knew him better than Helena did. Not only was Youwah proud, he was also stubborn. Nyeneplu simply nodded to her sister's suggestion rather than challenge Youwah's fake exhaustion.

"For true, I am tired," Youwah admitted, avoiding his wife's stare.

"Mr. Saytue, I hope that one day you will see that your strength may be your ability to see God's power and to trust Him," Pastor Peabody encouraged.

Youwah nodded, on account of being too tired to talk.

"Shall we pray then?" Pastor Peabody suggested.

"Yes," Helena and Nyeneplu answered.

Youwah made no answer. No one expected him to. Pastor Peabody, Helena and Nyeneplu bowed their heads and closed their eyes. Youwah widened his eyes in protest.

"God, we know you," Pastor Peabody began his prayer. "You hear the voice of those who truly listen to you. We beg for your pity because of our pride that makes us haughty, especially when we refuse to heed to Christ…Christ who has made atonement for us when we do not deserve it."

"Yes, Lord," Helena whispered, prayerfully.

Youwah looked at his sister-in-law and cut his eyes.

"God, please make us humble so we can know you," Pastor Peabody continued. "All power belongs to you…all glory belongs to you…

all things are in your hand; since the beginning of life here on Earth for all peoples, at all times. Everything and everyone are yours, God, until time itself will end."

"Yes, Lord," Helena whispered, prayerfully.

Youwah cut his eyes at his sister-in-law again. He shook his head this time.

"We beg you for rest from our burdens and we beg for the grace that we need," Pastor Peabody continued. "Lighten our toil, especially those that we must bear. Free us from our sins. At your name, Oh God, every knee must bow! At your son's name, Jesus Christ, every tongue must confess him, King! Only you, we are to worship…only you, we are to trust. Only you, God, we are to adore. So help us to leave all that is not holy and is not true. We invite you in our lives and we crown you king in our hearts."

"Yes, Lord," Helena and Nyeneplu whispered, prayerfully.

Youwah looked at his wife, then, his sister-in-law and sighed.

"Bless Youwah and Nyeneplu in their home and those that entered it," Pastor Peabody continued.

Youwah furrowed his brow when Pastor Peabody said his name.

"May your presence overpower any evil that comes here," Pastor Peabody went on. "God, I pray this prayer in your son's name, Jesus Christ. Amen."

"Amen!" Helena and Nyeneplu chorused.

"Ummm," Youwah mumbled. It was only to convince his wife of his efforts to cooperate.

"You know something, Mr. Saytue," Pastor Peabody advised, "God will open your eyes one day and you will see…everything false will disappear."

\*\*\*\*

After that day, it was a challenging two-week visit for Pastor Peabody and those catering to Youwah's needs; physical and spiritual. Youwah continued to fake exhaustion and sleep, depending on his attendant. Then, two weeks and a day later, the old Toyota pickup was packed up and Pastor Peabody and his passengers were ready to drive back to Montserrado. After saying farewell to Youwah, Pastor Peabody noticed Gyebo walking toward the back of the house and followed him there. He found the boy sobbing.

"Gyebo," Pastor Peabody called, touching the boy's shoulder.

Gyebo stopped crying. "Yes, Pastor," he answered calmly. He quickly wiped the tear stains off his face.

"You do not need to worry about your father," Pastor Peabody said. "You don't always have to be the one to ask God for something you need before He gives it. God allows us to pray for things for other people's needs."

The tears were dried now, and Gyebo's expression seemed a lot calmer.

"You believe me, don't you?" Pastor Peabody asked.

Gyebo nodded.

"Well," Pastor Peabody baited.

Gyebo mumbled, "That's not why I am crying."

"No," Pastor Peabody asked. "Would you like to tell me?"

There was a pause.

"Gyebo…maybe I can help."

"I do not want to go back to Monrovia," Gyebo confessed slyly.

"Did you ask your father if you could stay?"

"No."

"Why didn't you?"

"Because, Pastor, I know he won't let me."

"He would rather you went to school, wouldn't he?"

"Yes," Gyebo mumbled.

"Then, that's a good reason to go back," Pastor Peabody encouraged. "Don't worry about him, son…your father will be all right. I just know it."

****

After their guests drove away, Nyeneplu did not lighten up on her persuasion, or as Youwah called it, her harassment of God business. If only he could walk, he often thought, he'd run away from her. The fact was, Nyeneplu was his legs now. Then again, if God calls you to active duty, there is no telling; the prompting cannot be ignored. You don't want to risk being disobedient. Nyeneplu thought this to be her calling and she believed God wanted her to help her husband.

"There's a blessing in our suffering, Youwah," Nyeneplu started again. "That is the advantage in human weakness. When we are helpless, God's grace strengthens us."

Like a thorn in his side, Youwah could no longer bear it; meaning his life, the way things were. "Damn it, woman," he yelled, out of frustration. "It hurts bad enough without you poking at it."

This outburst startled Nyeneplu, bringing her to tears.

"All this blessing you are talking about, I'm the one who is suffering here, not you," Youwah shouted. "Where is the blessing? I cannot wash my own body without your help. If you don't bring me food, I will not eat. Tell me, Nyeneplu, where is the blessing in any of this?"

Nyeneplu touched her heart with her hand, trying to steady it. "I am your wife, Youwah, not just for the good times, but for the hard times as well," she pleaded tearfully. "When you are successful, I, too, am successful. When you are suffering, I am afflicted also. I'm feeling whatever you are feeling, Youwah. I pray every day for our comfort. One day it will come as we patiently endure the suffering."

Youwah felt the hurt in his wife's voice.

"Nyeneplu, I am so sorry," Youwah mumbled. "I feel as if I've received a death sentence…that's why I say these things."

"I understand," Nyeneplu whispered. "Like you, I am troubled, even beyond my faith. Even to the point where I sometimes despair life itself. Still, Youwah, I trust God. Our suffering is to make us rely on God, not on ourselves."

Youwah sighed, feeling like a beaten man.

"Please, Youwah," Nyeneplu pleaded.

"My dear wife, all these months you have been talking to God, nothing has happened," Youwah challenged. "By now, I know people in Pleebo have started talking behind your back. Don't you care?"

"I do not care, Youwah. Believe it or not, I'm not ashamed of my exhaustion," Nyeneplu protested. "God hears me. When the time comes, He will show me. Some things take time…God's time. The main thing is we must set our hope on God. Youwah, not just me…you too."

Youwah did not speak another word, for the sake of peace. Letting Nyeneplu have the last word was worth a restful night. Nyeneplu quietly prepared her husband for bed and settled in for the night.

****

Overwhelmed and worried with his problems, Youwah's soul felt parched and thirsty. He needed refreshment, if there is any for the spirit. He closed his eyes, but he was not sleeping. Then, he heard

Nyeneplu say, "Only God can calm our hearts, Youwah." Her voice sounded as if she was sitting right next to him. His wife's voice went on and on, repeating the same speech, until he could no longer hear his own thoughts. Youwah wished that God would quiet his mind so he couldn't hear her nagging. Her pleas became more pestering.

Youwah fell asleep but worry woke him. His eyes fluttered open to the still dark room. It was too early to get up. It seemed he was not even in rooster time yet. Youwah sighed, adjusted his covers, and hoped for sleep. He was staring at the ceiling when he should have been sleeping. Youwah stared for a long time, too long to know how long. He did not remember when, but sleep came and took over.

He could not tell how long he'd been sleeping, but Youwah's eyes opened, as if awakened from a deep sleep. It was as if all of his heart-breaks, disappointments and sadness had become intertwined with someone else's spirit. His spirit was like the spirit of a newborn baby, refreshing and blameless.

Youwah opened his mouth and found his voice calling for God's mercy. There was no anguish in it. Then, something had happened. Youwah regained full use of his legs, instantly. There was real muscle tone and strength that had been dead from inactivity for several months. The man believed he could walk again. "What!" Youwah cried.

Nyeneplu heard her husband's cry and ran to his room. She opened his bedroom door, saw her husband standing, and stopped. Nyeneplu stood in the doorway, wide-eye, looking at Youwah stand on his feet, confirming confidence.

"Youwah," Nyeneplu cried.

"Oh my God, Nyeneplu," Youwah cried, "Can you believe this?" He began rubbing his legs to reexamine the feelings he'd lost. He stomped his feet to test the energy of his new found leg. He jumped, giggling like a child. Youwah squatted and rose again. He stood on one leg, then the other, testing his knees. He marched ten steps in one direction, turned, and then walked back, all the time looking downward. For the first time in a very long time, since the accident, his legs were doing something his mind was telling them to do.

"Look, Nyeneplu, look…God did it," Youwah declared. "Oh God, let your Holy Spirit stay in my heart," he pounded his chest with his fist. "Nyeneplu, I want to destroy the things Geesayglocon gave me.

Destroy all the medicine, the juju…my *nyantono*[15] too. Yes, Nyeneplu, let God alone be in our home. Only God!"

"God alone," Nyeneplu asked.

"Only God," Youwah repeated. "God alone is great! God alone is good!"

"Youwah…Youwah," a whispery voice called.

Youwah opened his eyes and saw Nyeneplu standing over his bed, shaking him by his hip, to wake him. His breathing was fast and sweat dripped off him.

"Youwah," Nyeneplu called again, "You were talking in your sleep."

Youwah looked at his wife's face, reading worrisome on it.

"You were talking in your sleep," Nyeneplu repeated.

"What…what…what did I say," Youwah stammered.

"I didn't fully understand it," Nyeneplu lied. "Youwah, don't you remember it?"

Nyeneplu had heard him, but she wanted her husband to repeat God's name with his own mouth.

"No," Youwah shook his head.

Youwah had soldier everything in his life, but this was different. He had not cried since he was a small boy, now tears streamed down his face. What hurt Youwah, hurt Nyeneplu; his despairing bleats touched his wife's heart, filling it with pity. Nyeneplu sank near her husband, took his hand in hers and sat quietly.

After that night, Youwah did not discuss his dream with Nyeneplu or anyone else. His condition continued to stir him into giving up, but something inside his mind kept whispering, "Try it one more time, Youwah, try it one more time." If only Youwah would listen to that voice.

\*\*\*\*

Faith is not easy, especially when pride has built a nest in your heart. But when God is writing a story of faith through your life, the end is never in question. There's not much you can do, whether you know this or not. Despite your trials, the long weary path ends in God's arms.

The voice continued pouncing Youwah's conscience, '*Oh, Youwah, this fight is not yours, it is God's. Just because you think Geesayglocon is*

---

15    *Love medicine (potion) or substance thought to have magic power*

*wiser than you or he gives sweet speeches to persuade you, do not make him a god. Use the good sense God gave to you. After all, this is your life that you are gambling with, not the life of the man with the sweet tongue. Do not give God's glory to another. Do not praise any idol.'*

Truthfully, Youwah's soul fainted inside of him. He felt like the cowardly lion, unable to find his heart. He began to question his way. It looked good in his eyes, only his eyes, but it was taking him to death. If he stopped rejecting the idea of believing in God, maybe he would be blessed as Nyeneplu continued to suggest. He had fallen down with no help from Geesayglocon and his heart had no place to go, except ascend to God, Nyeneplu's *supernatural being* she had practically pushed down his throat.

"Only God can give the weary a calm and sweet repose," Nyeneplu preached to him over and over. "Only God can take you back to your desired place of safety."

"My ways no longer look good in my eyes," Youwah thought to himself. "How ridiculous am I to reject God because I think I know better. I do not know better."

Youwah considered a secret exit plan to seek a better completion for him. The only option was a final acceptance of the fact that God is real and God is everything. He would talk to God about his troubles because he was tired of trying to fool himself in doing things his way, a way to nowhere. In fact Youwah somehow understood why he had stumbled, as Nyeneplu had constantly put it. Youwah humbled himself before God, but wondered if God even wanted him. Perhaps his wife would know, he thought.

"Maybe I've gone too far now," Youwah admitted to his Nyeneplu. "There's no hope for a man like me, so there's no need to pray."

"That is not true, Youwah," Nyeneplu said. "God likes everybody, especially those who turn and come to Him. That's what Helena said their pastor told them."

"Really," Youwah said, in disbelief. "All the things you've accused me of doing, God will hear me?"

"Youwah, whatever we do, when we turn to God and ask for forgiveness, He will give us the opportunity for a new start. It is not God that you doubt, it's Geesayglocon. Are you afraid what may happen when Geesayglocon finds out you've thrown away his medicine?"

"Maybe," Youwah mumbled.

"Do not be afraid of any retaliation from him," Nyeneplu said. "No force is greater than the power of God. Only God is the strength of your life...of whom we must be afraid...only God."

There was a pause.

"Youwah Saytue, the God you do not want to respect raises the dead," Nyeneplu said, breaking the silence. "Don't you think God can make you walk?"

Youwah said nothing.

"What on earth can be too much for its Maker," Nyeneplu asked. "Nothing is greater than God."

Youwah collected his thoughts and asked, "Nyeneplu, all these things you are talking...where did it happen?"

"What things?"

"You said God made a man to live after he died...where in Pleebo did this thing happen?"

"I did not say it happened here in Pleebo," Nyeneplu corrected.

"Where in Liberia did it happen?"

"I did not say it happened in Liberia."

Youwah held his head in his hands and let his thoughts race through his mind. He debated in his mind whether to express his thoughts to Nyeneplu or not; he was not sure. The words percolated up into his consciousness, nearly making its way out of his lips. Rather than talk, Youwah would take in and let out a long, deep, audible breath. 'The dream seemed too real,' he wanted to tell her, but changed his mind. Youwah simply sat quietly with his head face-down in his hands.

"Youwah, say something," Nyeneplu encouraged, assuming her husband to be lost in thought.

A full sixty seconds passed, and then Youwah burst into a nervous laugh. This so-called cheeriness puzzled Nyeneplu and she forced out a chuckle, staring at him.

Youwah continued laughing.

"You do not believe me, do you," Nyeneplu asked.

"I believe you," Youwah managed to choke out.

"Then, why are you laughing?"

"Because this God business is too hard for some of us," Youwah confessed. "Sometimes I don't know if I'm dreaming or not dreaming."

Nyeneplu sensed her husband held a secret beneath his grin. If she treaded ever so carefully, she would know it. "I see," she whispered. "So, do you believe?"

"Believe what?"

"Believe that God can heal you."

"I don't know what to believe, Nyeneplu," Youwah admitted. "I just don't know.

Nyeneplu nodded, she understood his conflicting feelings towards his situation.

"All I know is, I want to put an end to this nonsense," Youwah said. "If this is God's handiwork, then let God's way be the way it ends."

"Let God finish it?" Nyeneplu asked.

"Yes."

"Okay, Youwah," Nyeneplu said, "let's leave it to God."

****

During the months after the accident, beyond the light housework, Nyeneplu was increasingly absorbed in making her kernel oil. She produced plenty to use and a surplus to sell. Gone were the days of sure cash-flow when Youwah was strong and in good physical shape. This did not bother Nyeneplu much, they had always made good on whatever they had available. She believed hard times were a reflection of her dependency on the loving God who had always bestowed so much of what she wished for and all of what she needed. As for the house in Montserrado, that could wait. This was what she told Youwah when he seemed worrisome about the concrete house and the shame he'd have to face if it could not be completed. The house walls were up, the windows sat at head-height, but there were no other means or plans to start the roof.

Youwah had not been able to walk on his own since the accident. To keep the blood flow in his legs going, Nyeneplu provided physical therapy for her husband, the way the doctor had taught her. The down side to the progress was Youwah's unwillingness to accept his dependency on others, especially his wife. To ease this uneasiness, Nyeneplu tried pampering him, at times arranging the therapy in a way where Youwah would lay with his feet in her lap. Youwah felt better, but halfway into the massage, he'd voice apologetic thoughts of his inability to continue to provide well for her. Hearing this, Nyeneplu would close her eyes and smile. She felt what they were going through was really testing her belief.

The number of visitors had also grown to be less than the time after the accident. Youwah had fallen into a loose pattern now—wake up late mornings, cleanup and dress with Nyeneplu's help, sit-up in a chair for an hour or so, eat dinner, curl up in bed for the rest of the day, then repeat the routine. It seemed Youwah's courage was melting away in the process of time, as if he was at his wit's end.

Laying in bed with not much to do, Youwah's thoughts often went back to the days when he worked more than ten hours a day; past the clearing of the paths to the palm oil trees deep in the forest where the land is unclaimed and unattended, past the high climb above Pleebo, past the cutting of palm nut bunches, past the chopping, boiling, beating, collecting of the red oil and filling of 5-gal containers to put up for sale. He reminisced about the first time he'd paid other men with money they earned to take care of their families. Youwah was especially proud of this. He was pleased that the market women were still buying red oil from Wakla, although not as much as before.

Five or six weeks had passed since Youwah's last meeting with his friend. They had exchanged accusations and distasteful words which had put tension on their friendship. Since then, Wakla had reported their business earnings direct to Nyeneplu instead of to Youwah. He'd also declined Nyeneplu's request, suggesting Wakla make the report to Youwah. Eventually, Wakla thought enough time had passed and wanted to mend the quarrel. Following his heart, he planned to visit with his old friend and it was not for business, just a mere visit.

After exchanging pleasantries with Nyeneplu, she directed Wakla to Youwah's room. A knock awoke Youwah and Wakla announced himself.

"Hello, Youwah," Wakla greeted his friend, but he was not sure of smiling.

"Hello!" Youwah answered. He was surprised and drowsy at the same time, yet smiling.

The exchange flowed soft and subtle, it seemed the tension between the friends had eased away to some extend. The two men actually felt good. Youwah pointed to a chair and Wakla sat in it.

"I would have come ever since, but I was waiting for your heart to sit down," Wakla confessed, as soon as his backside touched the seat of the chair.

Youwah raised his hand right away and said, "Please, Wakla, first thing first, I want to tell you I am sorry."

It was true, Youwah had ached for the friendship they once had. Wakla raised an eyebrow at his friend. He could not believe his ears.

"You win," Youwah said. Suggesting, but not admitting, he'd been wrong when he accused his friend of jealousy. "But listen," he continued in a more serious tone.

Wakla was pleased with Youwah's tone and he nodded.

Youwah cleared his throat and said, "I'm finished with Geesayglocon business."

"For true, Youwah?" Wakla asked.

"For true," Youwah repeated. "I don't need that kind of a useless man running my life. Nothing he has promised me has happened. I've overpaid him plenty times and all he says is, if God agrees. I'm tired of hearing that same promise; if God agrees, if God agrees. If Geesayglocon cannot make God to agree, why am I wasting my time with him for?"

Wakla's eyes widened with happiness.

"Besides, it's time now," Youwah continued. "I can no longer fight to keep my heart at ease. There is too much fear in it."

"Fear," Wakla said, in disbelief. "You have never spoken that word before, Youwah, since I've known you."

"I know…I know," Youwah admitted. "But you are hearing me say it now. I'm too scared."

"Is it Geesayglocon that you're afraid of?"

"No," Youwah shook his head.

"Then, who?"

"God," Youwah whispered.

"God," Wakla repeated, touching his heart. "Youwah, do you really fear God?"

"Yes-oh," Youwah said. "I fear God."

"Does Nyeneplu know this?"

"No," Youwah answered quickly. "You know how women are. That woman will never let me forget the fight I had with her about this God business. In fact, Wakla, it is all about the night I had a dream. That dream scared me."

"A dream," Wakla repeated. "What was it about?"

"Wakla, I cannot say it," Youwah said. "I am afraid to."

"Was God in it or what?"

"Only I was in it, but God was somewhere there teasing me," Youwah chuckled.

"Hmmm…," Wakla mused. "God was teasing you?"

"Wakla, that's how I see it-oh. God is teasing me."

"You are not making sense, Youwah, how so?"

"Wakla, I've had enough of it all. The experience of losing my dependency is too hard. I cannot fight it any longer. What will be, will be," Youwah said. "That's all I'm saying."

Wakla wondered what exactly had driven Youwah to such strong emotions about God now. But Youwah was not saying much. The issue seemed way beyond the man's face.

"Maybe we should change the topic," Wakla suggested, sensing it was hard for Youwah to explain the dream. Also, he did not want to risk another fight with his friend.

"We should," Youwah agreed, extending his hand for a handshake.

"You know something, Youwah," Wakla said, after the handshake. "Whether you agree with me or not, we are fit for our friendship. You've impressed me today like you've always done in the past."

Wakla's words were uplifting and Youwah smiled from ear to ear. It felt good knowing Wakla respected him still.

"Just so you know it, be ready for a change with this radical commitment," Wakla continued. "The one you're taking against Geesayglocon and his troubles. When God calls your name, it is not enough just to say you hear Him. Take it seriously when you answer and decide to follow. God business demands everything," he warned.

"Hmmm," Youwah voiced, not saying whether he would answer or not answer.

The remaining of the visit was spent bringing each other up to speed on the events that had happened since their fight. Wakla was doing his best to keep the oil business going and Youwah praised him for it. Youwah also commended his wife's service to him, which had helped him deal with his suffering. "Nyeneplu is a good woman," he bragged.

After the visit, Wakla went home glad and merry in his heart for his friend's about-turn in this new approach. Although Youwah had not fully admitted to following God, it seemed his heart had grown ears to hear. At least, he was seeking God's face, so Wakla thought.

****

Sure enough, Satan stood up against Youwah. The man had not expected it, but the devil appeared like he did in the garden.

The African black mamba is an eye catcher—to some Liberians, a bad luck or witchcraft—but certainly a venomous snake dreaded because of its quickness and readiness to bite. Its bite is often fatal, to say the least. Green and black mambas are one of the most dangerous and feared snakes in Africa. When you are standing in front of a black mamba hissing loudly, mouth gaping, striking rapidly in your direction, nothing is truer; your life flashes before your eyes. A single bite from a black mamba can inject enough venom to kill twenty grown men, easily killing one unless the proper anti-venom is administered in time. Rather than the skin color, the black mamba gets its name from the black coloration inside its mouth. The snake averages about 8 feet long and is known to be the fastest moving snake in the world, slithering at speeds of up to 12 miles per hour. When threatened, a mamba will readily attack. It was in this form the devil came to Youwah's home.

It was a quiet Friday evening after a delicious palm butter dinner, which Youwah had left mostly uneaten. Nyeneplu was bothered by this, but she did not make a fuss about it. Instead, she sat in a rattan chair, not too far from Youwah's bedroom window, mostly to watch the sun go down.

Time slipped by. Youwah and Nyeneplu talked very little. There was nothing to do except enjoy the laughter that spilled out now and then from different directions in the neighborhood and, of course, the rustling of palms swaying over Pleebo.

"Sometimes I can hear the palm nuts calling me, especially when it's breezy like that," Youwah said, looking at the opened bedroom window.

"Then, you must answer it," Nyeneplu replied in a soothing tone.

They both giggled as her words hung in the air for a moment or so.

"Hmmph," Youwah sighed. Then his gaze found its way from the window, down the wall and towards Nyeneplu's chair. Unmistakably he spotted it, the shiny black mamba, inches away from his wife.

"I am the person who challenged God, not Nyeneplu. I am to be punished, not Nyeneplu. Please God, let this evil pass from her,"

Youwah prayed.

Nyeneplu saw Youwah's lips move, but no sound came out of it. She thought nothing of it.

The lethal black mamba, now in striking position, flattened its neck, hissing loudly and displaying its inky black mouth and deadly fangs.

"Please, Nyeneplu, don't move," Youwah prayed in soft utterance.

The mamba moved at lightning speed.

"I tremble only before God and nothing else!" Youwah shouted. In that instant, he picked up his cutlass that was lying next to his bed. With cutlass raised above his head, Youwah got out of bed with lightning speed and struck the mamba with a single blow, slicing off its head.

It happened so fast, Nyeneplu only heard her husband in a soft whispery voice. She jumped to her feet, eyes widened, seeing Youwah standing. Then, she noticed the blood that was dripping off the blade of the knife onto the dead snake. "Youwah," she uttered softly, feeling chilled. Terror made her arms and legs to tremble. Nyeneplu realized what being bitten by the mamba would mean for her. Thank God, the death sentence had not reached her.

It was also at that moment, when Youwah realized not only was he standing; he had taken five giant steps to reach the snake. "One day, Youwah, God will open your eyes and you will see, everything false will disappear," he heard Pastor Peabody's voice clearly in his mind.

When asked about Youwah's miracle, much could not be explained.

"Some mysteries may never be understood,"Nyenelu simply replied.

****

Whatever you learn or know, teach it to somebody else. Sharing is a close neighbor of progress, especially when you find your purpose beyond yourself. Giving out portions of yourself is a choice, one that affirms life in all its forms, to either improve or to ruin. An amazing power lies in unselfishness, one man's willingness to share his map to success with his friend. It can plant hope in the lives of many others. Youwah Saytue's life had proven so.

Fifty or more people packed Youwah's yard to celebrate his miracle—neighbors, friends, relatives and strangers. A variety of foods, prepared by Nyeneplu and other women, were spread on small tables throughout the yard. They had jollof rice, white rice, potato greens, palm butter, roasted fish and roasted meat. One plastic table was topped with drinks—Fanta, Club Beer, palm wine, cane juice. A group of local cultural artists was also there to perform. More people were coming.

Wakla was first in line to praise Youwah and there was not a note of scorn in his voice. The guests were absorbed in the act of listening to the speaker. Wakla told of his friend's generosities, supporting dozens of people, some who were not even related to him, spooning them food. The success of their business had wrapped around more needy souls than he could actually count. All the good Youwah had done, it was the devil who wanted him harmed, not God.

"When you do good, you are spitting in the devil's face," Wakla told them. "The devil does not like that and that devil becomes your problem. However, God is greater than our greatest problem."

Then, wearing a kind expression on his face, Wakla praised his friend's new life and presented him a bright-colored African gown, one resembling that of a paramount chief. His eyes, shining with tranquility and energy, Wakla ended his speech, "Just because something is impossible doesn't mean you cannot believe in it. God is a healer. Thank you, God, for our brother, Youwah Saytue."

Many others gave small talk, mostly thanking God for Youwah's healing. Some praised Youwah for his help, the small-small loans to feed their family for a day or the money needed to buy medicine from the drugstore. Most never got repaid. Nyeneplu did not talk, only the men were voicing their thoughts. Then, it was Youwah's turn.

"This isn't the way I expected my life to be," Youwah said to his guests when he started. Then he asked, "What good can we get out of trials? It is hard to imagine it, isn't it?"

"Yes-oh," the audience confirmed together.

"And, sometimes the way in life seems impossibly steep and long and you have no strength or will for the journey," Youwah continued. "Instead of looking to God, you look to other people for guidance and comfort. But they are in that same boat, lost at sea with life's ups and downs. Not knowing, God is outside the boat and He is strong enough to calm the storms. God knew that road long before you were called to walk it. God has always known. He knows things that you or I can never explain to another person, not even your wife."

Many nodded in agreement.

"A man's heart plans the way to his future, but it is God who directs his steps," Youwah continued. "Many of you got to know part of my journey because of my accident. When that trouble came into my life, my wife kept telling me about God business. I reacted with anger. I could not understand why God, if He is good, would not take me to an easier road so I can find Him. Because of my wife's hardheadedness, she kept telling me, 'Youwah, we are not wise enough to know the correct way so God is showing you.'"

The audience laughed at Youwah's indication, clapping their hands, cheering. Some understood the journey, some understood hardheaded spouses, or the man's gesture was just funny. The cheer calmed and Youwah continued.

"The best thing I learned from all of this trouble is, God will never send you down the wrong path," Youwah urged. "Of all the possible roads, God knows the best way that will take you to the end. If any of you here are still trying to do things your way, thinking you know better, think again. Agree with God and go that way. Whatever our hopes and dreams are, when we place them in God's hands we know that everything, setback or success, is under His control." Youwah stopped, heaved a heavy sigh and choked, "God will be enough, but you must face that situation hand in hand with Him."

Youwah knelt on the bare earth and it was sort of a confession.

"I am just a simple man and nothing more," Youwah conceded, placing his hand over his chest. "God is in charge of my life now. He is my helper from yesterday and my hope for years to come." And then raising his hands toward heaven, he wailed, "God himself has placed His hands on me. Now I know…there is no life without suffering."

Youwah's confession, 'God is King in my heart,' triggered Nyeneplu's heart to pump pure liquid halleluiah into her bloodstreams. She made the sign of the cross over her heart and kissed her finger. Her beloved husband was out of an unrest and freed from an arrogant pride. God had heard her prayers.

A woman standing next to Nyeneplu asked, "Nyeneplu, is it God that took your husband out of his sickness? Do you really think God healed him in that dream? Do you believe it?"

Nyeneplu looked at the woman.

"Well…Nyeneplu, was it God?"

Nyeneplu sighed and said, "Good friend, when God gives you a break like that, you don't ask questions. You believe."

A picture book that offers a unique way to teach young children good manners using the 26 letters of the alphabets we all know. Each letter of the alphabet is represented, relating to teaching social standards with the principles of right conduct and good manner. Recommended for children ages 3 and up. Every parent should use this book, and every teacher too.

ISBN: 9780985362515
eISBN: 9780985362553
**Print and eBook**
Available from Amazon.com and
other retail outlets
Available on Kindle and other devices

Also available in 24 x 36
Jumbo Poster
www.villagetalespublishing.com

Read on for an excerpt from **DEAD GODS (HM2)**
By Ophelia S. Lewis

## 1

The world connects at lightning speed, but things were still as if it was 1986 in Liberia. After 15 years of civil war and six years of an elected presidency, progress was painfully slow. Although the cellular phone was booming and substantially more widespread than fixed line telephonic transmission, technology was otherwise, creeping out of the Stone Age in Monrovia—a city police department without computers on every detective's desk, and a wish list of working fax machines and photocopiers needed for critical documents. Forget quick access to DNA technology. Some would admit fingerprint was still being matched by human eye. All this is hard to gasp in today's CSI effect, but it is what it is.

His pay is not the biggest pay, his job is not the easiest, but Officer Lonos is a man who would rather die for his principals than live without one. He accepted the occupation as an officer knowing the responsibilities and hazards involved. As far as he was concerned, hell was not large enough for heart-men. Based on the most recent crime scene, it was evident the heart-men had struck again.

Behavior science never changes, so criminal profiling is still a quick thinker's investigative tool. For the detective in such environment, criminal profiling is always brought to the forefront of law enforcement. For one thing, such crime involves co-conspirators who could keep secrets. Secondly, logistics, the means of transportation. Getting from point A to point B increases having to be neat and discreet. Then, lodging the victim. They had to put their victim where extraction is done without drawing attention. Disposal was the final and easier step, Liberia's shorelines, the beaches.

As far as Lonos was concerned, Aaron Dolo had only done enough for his conscience to feel as if he had done something. The police chief had not done nearly enough because CeRue Manor, the mastermind behind most of the mishap in Monrovia, was still a loose thread.

It was no wonder that some consider victims of the heart-man unlucky. Murdering for human parts is a peculiar wicked deed, but a heart-man does his job and not cares about his soul. Keep in mind: heart-men are serial killers. Everyone takes part in a crime and everyone knows it's a crime except for the mastermind. As immoral as it is, CeRue Manor saw it as a business and made sure to keep it that way, buying and selling human parts as commodities. Lonos had yet to prove it.

The Good Book teaches: 'For the love of money is a root of all kinds of evils'. It is through this craving that some wander away from their conscience and does not experience anything close to a sharp pang of guilt. They push God completely out of their life, and set their hope on the uncertainty of riches. These kinds of people always want more because greed strengthens their hands. Lonos saw Manor as someone insatiable.

CeRue Manor had the sixth sense to foresee the rich future. Now that Liberia was about to dip her foot in oil, he vowed to play a key role in it too. He was doing well, more than well. His wheeling and dealing concealed some of the biggest unlicensed business operations in Africa that made millions—the smuggling of diamonds, underage girls, and human organs. Since kickbacks and corruption turn a blind eye to regulations, smuggling paid exuberantly well, along with illegitimate private clubs.

If there was a place where people could meet with reasonable confidence that their deeds would not be exposed even in their world of ultra sophisticated matters of illegal, or even murderous, it was Manor's exclusive club, Le'Toit, (English translation-The Rooftop), a facility not for public. No one set foot in some areas and it was Manor who prescribed limits for his establishment. Even his trusted acquaintances went so far, and not further. Le'Toit was surrounded by hidden security cameras, and only Manor knew their locations.

'A fool's paradise', that's what Lynnette Vinton, aka Salvation Lady, calls the club, but services were premium all the way. "Satan is in the walls of that place," she often said.

Activities at Le'Toit was not limited to just a place where rich men met and drank, organized prostitution soared. Underage girls, barely teenage, were shipped in from neighboring counties to entertain these men. They had not come on their own, most being kidnapped. His assistant, an Ivorian native, handled all Manor's commodities, directing the routes of his precious freights—girls, human organs, drugs, diamonds, and weapons.

Inside the naughty housing of Le'Toit, amid the drinking, gambling and businessmen chatting their wheeling and dealing, the winding hall led to a place where a darker side of Manor's financial bloom lies, the top floor. Young girls are kept here to satisfy the men's lusts. The girls are forced to have sex with men for long hours, and are denied contact with anyone, family or others. Some were put into an international placement agency for mail-order brides. Human trafficking by unregulated placement agencies for maids, rather than prostitutes, was also a part of Manor's business. Demand for maids was increasing because in America and Europe, people would pay far less for what they would normally pay legal agencies for people to cook, clean, and look after their children.

Manor did not employ stupid people either, and his employees were compensated very well. Over half of his staff were imported into Liberia and they all had one thing in common; convicted criminal. He made sure all his well qualified employees had salaries bumped way higher than their counterparts, paying them far more than they'd earned any place else. His medical team was structured with an Asian doctor, an Indian surgeon, a Jamaican bartender, and a head waitress named Peaches.

Peaches had worked Las Vegas five years before coming to work for Manor. Wild as hell, she had spent more time in the backseat of cars than she did in the classroom, could drink any man under the table, and always had a purse full of pills. Other than her legal documents, passport or driver license, Peaches didn't need a last name.

Cheah Boatswain, a Monrovia city police officer, ran Manor's personal security force. Once a war lord, Boatswain was one of those who tried to make a holocaust out of Liberia all at once, fueling the senseless civil war with acts of violence beyond wordy description. Most remembered the mad killer, a short man with a shaven head and bushy beard. Though Boatswain had grown his hair and shaved his beard, people remembered him.

A civil war had been ignited because a few Liberian men turned war lords, set their minds on reversing peaceful living to war time so they could take ownership of things they did not want to work for. To rule you must serve, but their mixed-up instincts, and sneaking urge to power, permitted them to rule and get fancy cars and big houses they did not pay for. They turned from being family guards to become gun smugglers' customers who turned them into dogs. They sold drugs along with the country resources, like timbers and diamonds. They put guns and drugs into the hands of their sons and taught them to be rapists and murderers. The assaults on women were inconceivable, as if these men had never clinched to breasts that nourished them.

Today, lawless killings were in the past. But like every place in the world, crime still soared in Liberia.

## READ ALL THE HEART MEN BOOKS

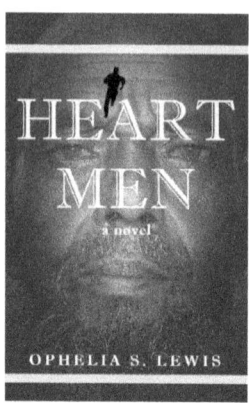 

**HEART MEN** (a novel)
Paperback / 244 Pages / 2011
ISBN 13: 9780975360965
eBook ISBN: 9780975360996

**DEAD GODS** (HM2)
Paperback / 396 Pages / 2014
ISBN 13: 9780978362522
eBook ISBN: 9780978362539

### READERS REVIEWS

"I am REALLY ENJOYING Heart Men..."—*Richelle Howell*

"Overall, HEART MEN is an INTERESTING read...I ENJOYED RJ's PASSION for life, his LOVE for his family, and his tenacious search for the TRUTH...I certainly enjoyed his story. It held my interest from beginning to end."—Damali Griffin (Imani Literary Group Book Club Member)

"This is a story that has NEVER BEEN TOLD...I was pleasantly surprised to find out it is a LOVE STORY more than anything..."—Manseen Logan (Bella Beau Marketing & Publicity)

"I just finished reading HEART MEN here in Ghana on my Kindle...I LIKED IT A LOT...It seems that there are so many TABOO SUBJECTS in a society, and this is one not just in Liberia but everywhere...—Tim Nevin

# About the Author

*Photo by Portia Langley*

## Ophelia S. Lewis

Lewis is a poet, essayist, and a creative writer. Since early childhood she loved dramatic arts, and in 2011 plucked up the courage to put pen to paper with her first novel, Heart Men. While Lewis is determined to make Village Tales Publishing a recognized name in the literary industry, she has written and published three children's books, a book of poetry, a book of essay and two collections of short stories, with the latest being Montserrado Stories.

Lewis lives with her family in the State of Georgia.

www.ingramcontent.com/pod-product-compliance
Lightning Source LLC
Chambersburg PA
CBHW071947170626
46813CB00005B/1861